Late Lyrics and Earlier

With Many Other Verses

Thomas Hardy

Late Lyrics and Earlier, With Many Other Verses

The present edition is a reproduction of previous publication of this classic work. Minor typographical errors may have been corrected without note; however, for an authentic reading experience the spelling, punctuation, and capitalization have been retained from the original text.

ISBN: 978-1-63637-950-0

CONTENTS

APOLOGY

About half the verses that follow were written quite lately. The rest are older, having been held over in MS. when past volumes were published, on considering that these would contain a sufficient number of pages to offer readers at one time, more especially during the distractions of the war. The unusually far back poems to be found here are, however, but some that were overlooked in gathering previous collections. A freshness in them, now unattainable, seemed to make up for their inexperience and to justify their inclusion. A few are dated; the dates of others are not discoverable.

The launching of a volume of this kind in neo-Georgian days by one who began writing in mid-Victorian, and has published nothing to speak of for some years, may seem to call for a few words of excuse or explanation. Whether or no, readers may feel assured that a new book is submitted to them with great hesitation at so belated a date. Insistent practical reasons, however, among which were requests from some illustrious men of letters who are in sympathy with my productions, the accident that several of the poems have already seen the light, and that dozens of them have been lying about for years, compelled the course adopted, in spite of the natural disinclination of a writer whose works have been so frequently regarded askance by a pragmatic section here and there, to draw attention to them once more.

I do not know that it is necessary to say much on the contents of the book, even in deference to suggestions that will be mentioned presently. I believe that those readers who care for my poems at all—readers to whom no passport is required—will care for this new instalment of them, perhaps the last, as much as for any that have preceded them. Moreover, in the eyes of a less friendly class the pieces, though a very mixed collection indeed, contain, so far as I am able to see, little or nothing in technic or teaching that can be considered a Star-Chamber matter, or so much as agitating to a ladies' school; even though, to use Wordsworth's observation in his Preface to Lyrical Ballads, such readers may suppose "that by the act of writing in verse an author makes a formal engagement that he will gratify certain known habits of association: that he not only thus apprises the reader that certain classes of ideas and expressions will be found in his book, but that others will be carefully excluded."

It is true, nevertheless, that some grave, positive, stark,

delineations are interspersed among those of the passive, lighter, and traditional sort presumably nearer to stereotyped tastes. For—while I am quite aware that a thinker is not expected, and, indeed, is scarcely allowed, now more than heretofore, to state all that crosses his mind concerning existence in this universe, in his attempts to explain or excuse the presence of evil and the incongruity of penalizing the irresponsible—it must be obvious to open intelligences that, without denying the beauty and faithful service of certain venerable cults, such disallowance of "obstinate questionings" and "blank misgivings" tends to a paralysed intellectual stalemate. Heine observed nearly a hundred years ago that the soul has her eternal rights; that she will not be darkened by statutes, nor lullabied by the music of bells. And what is to-day, in allusions to the present author's pages, alleged to be "pessimism" is, in truth, only such "questionings" in the exploration of reality, and is the first step towards the soul's betterment, and the body's also.

If I may be forgiven for quoting my own old words, let me repeat what I printed in this relation more than twenty years ago, and wrote much earlier, in a poem entitled "In Tenebris":

If way to the Better there be, it exacts a full look at the Worst:

that is to say, by the exploration of reality, and its frank recognition stage by stage along the survey, with an eye to the best consummation possible: briefly, evolutionary meliorism. But it is called pessimism nevertheless; under which word, expressed with condemnatory emphasis, it is regarded by many as some pernicious new thing (though so old as to underlie the Christian idea, and even to permeate the Greek drama); and the subject is charitably left to decent silence, as if further comment were needless.

Happily there are some who feel such Levitical passing-by to be, alas, by no means a permanent dismissal of the matter; that comment on where the world stands is very much the reverse of needless in these disordered years of our prematurely afflicted century: that amendment and not madness lies that way. And looking down the future these few hold fast to the same: that whether the human and kindred animal races survive till the exhaustion or destruction of the globe, or whether these races perish and are succeeded by others before that conclusion comes, pain to all upon it, tongued or dumb, shall be kept down to a minimum by lovingkindness, operating through scientific knowledge, and actuated by the modicum of free will conjecturally possessed by organic life when the mighty necessitating forces—

unconscious or other—that have "the balancings of the clouds," happen to be in equilibrium, which may or may not be often.

To conclude this question I may add that the argument of the so-called optimists is neatly summarized in a stern pronouncement against me by my friend Mr. Frederic Harrison in a late essay of his, in the words: "This view of life is not mine." The solemn declaration does not seem to me to be so annihilating to the said "view" (really a series of fugitive impressions which I have never tried to co-ordinate) as is complacently assumed. Surely it embodies a too human fallacy quite familiar in logic. Next, a knowing reviewer, apparently a Roman Catholic young man, speaks, with some rather gross instances of the suggestio falsi in his article, of "Mr. Hardy refusing consolation," the "dark gravity of his ideas," and so on. When a Positivist and a Catholic agree there must be something wonderful in it, which should make a poet sit up. But . . . O that 'twere possible!

I would not have alluded in this place or anywhere else to such casual personal criticisms—for casual and unreflecting they must be—but for the satisfaction of two or three friends in whose opinion a short answer was deemed desirable, on account of the continual repetition of these criticisms, or more precisely, quizzings. After all, the serious and truly literary inquiry in this connection is: Should a shaper of such stuff as dreams are made on disregard considerations of what is customary and expected, and apply himself to the real function of poetry, the application of ideas to life (in Matthew Arnold's familiar phrase)? This bears more particularly on what has been called the "philosophy" of these poems—usually reproved as "queer." Whoever the author may be that undertakes such application of ideas in this "philosophic" direction—where it is specially required—glacial judgments must inevitably fall upon him amid opinion whose arbiters largely decry individuality, to whom ideas are oddities to smile at, who are moved by a yearning the reverse of that of the Athenian inquirers on Mars Hill; and stiffen their features not only at sound of a new thing, but at a restatement of old things in new terms. Hence should anything of this sort in the following adumbrations seem "queer"—should any of them seem to good Panglossians to embody strange and disrespectful conceptions of this best of all possible worlds, I apologize; but cannot help it.

Such divergences, which, though piquant for the nonce, it would be affectation to say are not saddening and discouraging likewise, may, to be sure, arise sometimes from superficial aspect only, writer and reader seeing the same thing at different angles. But in palpable cases of divergence they arise, as already said, whenever a serious effort is made towards that which the authority I have cited—who would now be called old-fashioned, possibly even parochial—affirmed to be what no good critic could deny as the poet's province, the application of ideas to life. One might shrewdly guess, by the by, that in such recommendation the famous writer may have overlooked the cold-shouldering results upon an enthusiastic disciple that would be pretty certain to follow his putting the high aim in practice, and have forgotten the disconcerting experience of Gil Blas with the Archbishop.

To add a few more words to what has already taken up too many, there is a contingency liable to miscellanies of verse that I have never seen mentioned, so far as I can remember; I mean the chance little shocks that may be caused over a book of various character like the present and its predecessors by the juxtaposition of unrelated, even discordant, effusions; poems perhaps years apart in the making, yet facing each other. An odd result of this has been that dramatic anecdotes of a satirical and humorous intention (such, e.g., as "Royal Sponsors") following verse in graver voice, have been read as misfires because they raise the smile that they were intended to raise, the journalist, deaf to the sudden change of key, being unconscious that he is laughing with the author and not at him. I admit that I did not foresee such contingencies as I ought to have done, and that people might not perceive when the tone altered. But the difficulties of arranging the themes in a graduated kinship of moods would have been so great that irrelation was almost unavoidable with efforts so diverse. I must trust for right note-catching to those finely-touched spirits who can divine without half a whisper, whose intuitiveness is proof against all the accidents of inconsequence. In respect of the less alert, however, should any one's train of thought be thrown out of gear by a consecutive piping of vocal reeds in jarring tonics, without a semiquaver's rest between, and be led thereby to miss the writer's aim and meaning in one out of two contiguous compositions, I shall deeply regret it.

Having at last, I think, finished with the personal points that I was recommended to notice, I will forsake the immediate object of this Preface; and, leaving Late Lyrics to whatever fate it deserves, digress for a few moments to more general considerations. The thoughts of any man of letters concerned to keep poetry alive cannot but run uncomfortably on the precarious prospects of English verse at the present day. Verily the hazards and casualties surrounding the birth and setting forth of almost every modern creation in numbers are ominously like those of one of Shelley's paper-boats on a windy lake. And a forward conjecture scarcely permits the hope of a better time, unless men's tendencies should change. So indeed of all art, literature, and "high thinking" nowadays. Whether owing to the barbarizing of taste in the younger minds by the dark madness of the late war, the unabashed cultivation of selfishness in all classes, the plethoric growth of knowledge simultaneously with the stunting of wisdom, "a degrading thirst after outrageous stimulation" (to quote Wordsworth again), or from any other cause, we seem threatened with a new Dark Age.

I formerly thought, like so many roughly handled writers, that so far as literature was concerned a partial cause might be impotent or mischievous criticism; the satirizing of individuality, the lack of whole-seeing in contemporary estimates of poetry and kindred work, the knowingness affected by junior reviewers, the overgrowth of meticulousness in their peerings for an opinion, as if it were a cultivated habit in them to scrutinize the tool-marks and be blind to the building, to hearken for the key-creaks and be deaf to the diapason, to judge the landscape by a nocturnal exploration with a flash-lantern. In other words, to carry on the old game of sampling the poem or drama by quoting the worst line or worst passage only, in ignorance or not of Coleridge's proof that a versification of any length neither can be nor ought to be all poetry; of reading meanings into a book that its author never dreamt of writing there. I might go on interminably.

But I do not now think any such temporary obstructions to be the cause of the hazard, for these negligences and ignorances, though they may have stifled a few true poets in the run of generations, disperse like stricken leaves before the wind of next week, and are no more heard of again in the region of letters than their writers themselves. No: we may be convinced that something of the deeper sort mentioned must be the cause.

In any event poetry, pure literature in general, religion—I include religion because poetry and religion touch each other, or rather modulate into each other; are, indeed, often but different names for the same thing—these, I say, the visible signs of mental and emotional life, must like all other things keep moving, becoming; even though at present, when belief in witches of Endor is displacing the Darwinian theory and "the truth that shall make you free," men's minds appear, as above noted, to be moving backwards rather than on. I speak, of course, somewhat sweepingly, and should except many isolated minds; also the minds of men in certain worthy but small bodies of various denominations, and perhaps in the homely quarter where advance might have been the very least expected a few years back—the English Church—if one reads it rightly as showing evidence of "removing those things that are shaken," in accordance with the wise Epistolary recommendation to the Hebrews. For since the historic and once august hierarchy of Rome some generation ago lost its chance of being the religion of the future by doing otherwise, and throwing over the little band of neo-Catholics who were making a struggle for continuity by applying the principle of evolution to their own faith, joining hands with modern science, and outflanking the hesitating English instinct towards liturgical reform (a flank march which I at the time quite expected to witness, with the gathering of many millions of waiting agnostics into its fold); since then, one may ask, what other purely English establishment than the Church, of sufficient dignity and footing, and with such strength of old association, such architectural spell, is left in this country to keep the shreds of morality together?

It may be a forlorn hope, a mere dream, that of an alliance between religion, which must be retained unless the world is to perish, and complete rationality, which must come, unless also the world is to perish, by means of the interfusing effect of poetry—"the breath and finer spirit of all knowledge; the impassioned expression of science," as it was defined by an English poet who was quite orthodox in his ideas. But if it be true, as Comte argued, that advance is never in a straight line, but in a looped orbit, we may, in the aforesaid ominous moving backward, be doing it pour mieux sauter, drawing back for a spring. I repeat that I forlornly hope so, notwithstanding the supercilious regard of hope by Schopenhauer, von Hartmann, and other philosophers down to Einstein who have my respect. But one dares not prophesy. Physical, chronological, and other contingencies keep me in these days from critical studies and literary circles

Where once we held debate, a band
Of youthful friends, on mind and art

(if one may quote Tennyson in this century of free verse). Hence I cannot know how things are going so well as I used to know them, and the aforesaid limitations must quite prevent my knowing hence-forward.

I have to thank the editors and owners of The Times, Fortnightly, Mercury, and other periodicals in which a few of the poems have appeared for kindly assenting to their being reclaimed for collected publication.

T. H.
February 1922

WEATHERS

I

This is the weather the cuckoo likes,
  And so do I;
When showers betumble the chestnut spikes,
  And nestlings fly:
And the little brown nightingale bills his best,
And they sit outside at "The Travellers' Rest,"
And maids come forth sprig-muslin drest,
And citizens dream of the south and west,
  And so do I.

II

This is the weather the shepherd shuns,
  And so do I;
When beeches drip in browns and duns,
  And thresh, and ply;
And hill-hid tides throb, throe on throe,
And meadow rivulets overflow,
And drops on gate-bars hang in a row,
And rooks in families homeward go,
  And so do I.

THE MAID OF KEINTON MANDEVILLE

(A TRIBUTE TO SIR H. BISHOP)

I hear that maiden still
Of Keinton Mandeville
Singing, in flights that played
As wind-wafts through us all,
Till they made our mood a thrall
To their aery rise and fall,

"Should he upbraid."
Rose-necked, in sky-gray gown,
From a stage in Stower Town
Did she sing, and singing smile
As she blent that dexterous voice
With the ditty of her choice,
And banished our annoys
   Thereawhile.

One with such song had power
To wing the heaviest hour
Of him who housed with her.
Who did I never knew
When her spoused estate ondrew,
And her warble flung its woo
   In his ear.

Ah, she's a beldame now,
Time-trenched on cheek and brow,
Whom I once heard as a maid
From Keinton Mandeville
Of matchless scope and skill
Sing, with smile and swell and trill,
   "Should he upbraid!"

1915 or 1916

SUMMER SCHEMES

When friendly summer calls again,
   Calls again
Her little fifers to these hills,
We'll go—we two—to that arched fane
Of leafage where they prime their bills
Before they start to flood the plain
With quavers, minims, shakes, and trills.
   "—We'll go," I sing; but who shall say
   What may not chance before that day!

And we shall see the waters spring,
   Waters spring
From chinks the scrubby copses crown;
And we shall trace their oncreeping
To where the cascade tumbles down
And sends the bobbing growths aswing,
And ferns not quite but almost drown.
   "—We shall," I say; but who may sing
   Of what another moon will bring!

EPEISODIA

I

Past the hills that peep
Where the leaze is smiling,
On and on beguiling
Crisply-cropping sheep;
Under boughs of brushwood
Linking tree and tree
In a shade of lushwood,
   There caressed we!

II

Hemmed by city walls
That outshut the sunlight,
In a foggy dun light,
Where the footstep falls
With a pit-pat wearisome
In its cadency
On the flagstones drearisome
   There pressed we!

III

Where in wild-winged crowds

Blown birds show their whiteness
Up against the lightness
Of the clammy clouds;
By the random river
Pushing to the sea,
Under bents that quiver
  There rest we.

FAINTHEART IN A RAILWAY TRAIN

At nine in the morning there passed a church,
  At ten there passed me by the sea,
At twelve a town of smoke and smirch,
At two a forest of oak and birch,
  And then, on a platform, she:

A radiant stranger, who saw not me.
I queried, "Get out to her do I dare?"
But I kept my seat in my search for a plea,
And the wheels moved on. O could it but be
  That I had alighted there!

AT MOONRISE AND ONWARDS

I thought you a fire
On Heron-Plantation Hill,
Dealing out mischief the most dire
To the chattels of men of hire
There in their vill.

But by and by
You turned a yellow-green,
Like a large glow-worm in the sky;

And then I could descry
Your mood and mien.

How well I know
Your furtive feminine shape!
As if reluctantly you show
You nude of cloud, and but by favour throw
Aside its drape . . .

—How many a year
Have you kept pace with me,
Wan Woman of the waste up there,
Behind a hedge, or the bare
Bough of a tree!

No novelty are you,
O Lady of all my time,
Veering unbid into my view
Whether I near Death's mew,
Or Life's top cyme!

THE GARDEN SEAT

Its former green is blue and thin,
And its once firm legs sink in and in;
Soon it will break down unaware,
Soon it will break down unaware.

At night when reddest flowers are black
Those who once sat thereon come back;
Quite a row of them sitting there,
Quite a row of them sitting there.

With them the seat does not break down,
Nor winter freeze them, nor floods drown,
For they are as light as upper air,
They are as light as upper air!

BARTHÉLÉMON AT VAUXHALL

François Hippolite Barthélémon, first-fiddler at Vauxhall Gardens, composed what was probably the most popular morning hymn-tune ever written. It was formerly sung, full-voiced, every Sunday in most churches, to Bishop Ken's words, but is now seldom heard.

He said: "Awake my soul, and with the sun," . . .
And paused upon the bridge, his eyes due east,
Where was emerging like a full-robed priest
The irradiate globe that vouched the dark as done.

It lit his face—the weary face of one
Who in the adjacent gardens charged his string,
Nightly, with many a tuneful tender thing,
Till stars were weak, and dancing hours outrun.

And then were threads of matin music spun
In trial tones as he pursued his way:
"This is a morn," he murmured, "well begun:
This strain to Ken will count when I am clay!"

And count it did; till, caught by echoing lyres,
It spread to galleried naves and mighty quires.

"I SOMETIMES THINK"

(FOR F. E. H.)

I sometimes think as here I sit
Of things I have done,
Which seemed in doing not unfit
To face the sun:
Yet never a soul has paused a whit
On such—not one.

There was that eager strenuous press

To sow good seed;
There was that saving from distress
In the nick of need;
There were those words in the wilderness:
Who cared to heed?

Yet can this be full true, or no?
For one did care,
And, spiriting into my house, to, fro,
Like wind on the stair,
Cares still, heeds all, and will, even though
I may despair.

JEZREEL

ON ITS SEIZURE BY THE ENGLISH UNDER ALLENBY, SEPTEMBER 1918

Did they catch as it were in a Vision at shut of the day—
When their cavalry smote through the ancient Esdraelon Plain,
And they crossed where the Tishbite stood forth in his enemy's way—
His gaunt mournful Shade as he bade the King haste off amain?

On war-men at this end of time—even on Englishmen's eyes—
Who slay with their arms of new might in that long-ago place,
Flashed he who drove furiously? . . . Ah, did the phantom arise
Of that queen, of that proud Tyrian woman who painted her face?

Faintly marked they the words "Throw her down!" rise from Night eerily,
Spectre-spots of the blood of her body on some rotten wall?
And the thin note of pity that came: "A King's daughter is she,"
As they passed where she trodden was once by the chargers' footfall?

Could such be the hauntings of men of to-day, at the cease
Of pursuit, at the dusk-hour, ere slumber their senses could seal?

Enghosted seers, kings—one on horseback who asked "Is it peace?"...
Yea, strange things and spectral may men have beheld in Jezreel!

September 24, 1918

A JOG-TROT PAIR

Who were the twain that trod this track
So many times together
Hither and back,
In spells of certain and uncertain weather?
Commonplace in conduct they
Who wandered to and fro here
Day by day:
Two that few dwellers troubled themselves to know here.

The very gravel-path was prim
That daily they would follow:
Borders trim:
Never a wayward sprout, or hump, or hollow.

Trite usages in tamest style
Had tended to their plighting.
"It's just worth while,
Perhaps," they had said. "And saves much sad good-nighting."

And petty seemed the happenings
That ministered to their joyance:
Simple things,
Onerous to satiate souls, increased their buoyance.

Who could those common people be,
Of days the plainest, barest?
They were we;
Yes; happier than the cleverest, smartest, rarest.

"THE CURTAINS NOW ARE DRAWN"

(SONG)

I

The curtains now are drawn,
And the spindrift strikes the glass,
Blown up the jagged pass
By the surly salt sou'-west,
And the sneering glare is gone
Behind the yonder crest,
   While she sings to me:
"O the dream that thou art my Love, be it thine,
And the dream that I am thy Love, be it mine,
And death may come, but loving is divine."

II

I stand here in the rain,
   With its smite upon her stone,
   And the grasses that have grown
   Over women, children, men,
   And their texts that "Life is vain";
   But I hear the notes as when
      Once she sang to me:
"O the dream that thou art my Love, be it thine,
And the dream that I am thy Love, be it mine,
And death may come, but loving is divine."

1913

"ACCORDING TO THE MIGHTY WORKING"

I

When moiling seems at cease
  In the vague void of night-time,
  And heaven's wide roomage stormless
  Between the dusk and light-time,
  And fear at last is formless,
We call the allurement Peace.

II

Peace, this hid riot, Change,
  This revel of quick-cued mumming,
  This never truly being,
  This evermore becoming,
  This spinner's wheel onfleeing
Outside perception's range.

1917

"I WAS NOT HE"

(SONG)

I was not he—the man
Who used to pilgrim to your gate,
At whose smart step you grew elate,
And rosed, as maidens can,
  For a brief span.

It was not I who sang
Beside the keys you touched so true
With note-bent eyes, as if with you

10

It counted not whence sprang
The voice that rang . . .

Yet though my destiny
It was to miss your early sweet,
You still, when turned to you my feet,
Had sweet enough to be
A prize for me!

THE WEST-OF-WESSEX GIRL

A very West-of-Wessex girl,
As blithe as blithe could be,
Was once well-known to me,
And she would laud her native town,
And hope and hope that we
Might sometime study up and down
Its charms in company.

But never I squired my Wessex girl
In jaunts to Hoe or street
When hearts were high in beat,
Nor saw her in the marbled ways
Where market-people meet
That in her bounding early days
Were friendly with her feet.

Yet now my West-of-Wessex girl,
When midnight hammers slow
From Andrew's, blow by blow,
As phantom draws me by the hand
To the place—Plymouth Hoe—
Where side by side in life, as planned,
We never were to go!

Begun in Plymouth, March 1913

WELCOME HOME

To my native place
Bent upon returning,
Bosom all day burning
To be where my race
Well were known, 'twas much with me
There to dwell in amity.

Folk had sought their beds,
But I hailed: to view me
Under the moon, out to me
Several pushed their heads,
And to each I told my name,
Plans, and that therefrom I came.

"Did you? . . . Ah, 'tis true
I once heard, back a long time,
Here had spent his young time,
Some such man as you . . .
Good-night." The casement closed again,
And I was left in the frosty lane.

GOING AND STAYING

I

The moving sun-shapes on the spray,
The sparkles where the brook was flowing,
Pink faces, plightings, moonlit May,
These were the things we wished would stay;
  But they were going.

II

Seasons of blankness as of snow,
The silent bleed of a world decaying,

The moan of multitudes in woe,
These were the things we wished would go;
  But they were staying.

III

Then we looked closelier at Time,
And saw his ghostly arms revolving
To sweep off woeful things with prime,
Things sinister with things sublime
  Alike dissolving.

READ BY MOONLIGHT

I paused to read a letter of hers
  By the moon's cold shine,
Eyeing it in the tenderest way,
And edging it up to catch each ray
  Upon her light-penned line.
I did not know what years would flow
  Of her life's span and mine
Ere I read another letter of hers
  By the moon's cold shine!

I chance now on the last of hers,
  By the moon's cold shine;
It is the one remaining page
Out of the many shallow and sage
  Whereto she set her sign.
Who could foresee there were to be
  Such letters of pain and pine
Ere I should read this last of hers
  By the moon's cold shine!

AT A HOUSE IN HAMPSTEAD

SOMETIME THE DWELLING OF JOHN KEATS

O poet, come you haunting here
Where streets have stolen up all around,
And never a nightingale pours one
Full-throated sound?

Drawn from your drowse by the Seven famed Hills,
Thought you to find all just the same
Here shining, as in hours of old,
If you but came?

What will you do in your surprise
At seeing that changes wrought in Rome
Are wrought yet more on the misty slope
One time your home?

Will you wake wind-wafts on these stairs?
Swing the doors open noisily?
Show as an umbraged ghost beside
Your ancient tree?

Or will you, softening, the while
You further and yet further look,
Learn that a laggard few would fain
Preserve your nook? . . .

—Where the Piazza steps incline,
And catch late light at eventide,
I once stood, in that Rome, and thought,
"'Twas here he died."

I drew to a violet-sprinkled spot,
Where day and night a pyramid keeps
Uplifted its white hand, and said,
"'Tis there he sleeps."

Pleasanter now it is to hold
That here, where sang he, more of him

Remains than where he, tuneless, cold,
    Passed to the dim.

July 1920

A WOMAN'S FANCY

"Ah Madam; you've indeed come back here?
    'Twas sad—your husband's so swift death,
And you away! You shouldn't have left him:
    It hastened his last breath."

"Dame, I am not the lady you think me;
    I know not her, nor know her name;
I've come to lodge here—a friendless woman;
    My health my only aim."

She came; she lodged. Wherever she rambled
    They held her as no other than
The lady named; and told how her husband
    Had died a forsaken man.

So often did they call her thuswise
    Mistakenly, by that man's name,
So much did they declare about him,
    That his past form and fame

Grew on her, till she pitied his sorrow
    As if she truly had been the cause—
Yea, his deserter; and came to wonder
    What mould of man he was.

"Tell me my history!" would exclaim she;
    "Our history," she said mournfully.
"But you know, surely, Ma'am?" they would answer,
    Much in perplexity.

Curious, she crept to his grave one evening,
    And a second time in the dusk of the morrow;

Then a third time, with crescent emotion
Like a bereaved wife's sorrow.

No gravestone rose by the rounded hillock;
—"I marvel why this is?" she said.
—"He had no kindred, Ma'am, but you near."
—She set a stone at his head.

She learnt to dream of him, and told them:
"In slumber often uprises he,
And says: 'I am joyed that, after all, Dear,
You've not deserted me!"

At length died too this kinless woman,
As he had died she had grown to crave;
And at her dying she besought them
To bury her in his grave.

Such said, she had paused; until she added:
"Call me by his name on the stone,
As I were, first to last, his dearest,
Not she who left him lone!"

And this they did. And so it became there
That, by the strength of a tender whim,
The stranger was she who bore his name there,
Not she who wedded him.

HER SONG

I sang that song on Sunday,
To witch an idle while,
I sang that song on Monday,
As fittest to beguile;
I sang it as the year outwore,
And the new slid in;
I thought not what might shape before
Another would begin.

16

I sang that song in summer,
All unforeknowingly,
To him as a new-comer
From regions strange to me:
I sang it when in afteryears
The shades stretched out,
And paths were faint; and flocking fears
Brought cup-eyed care and doubt.

Sings he that song on Sundays
In some dim land afar,
On Saturdays, or Mondays,
As when the evening star
Glimpsed in upon his bending face
And my hanging hair,
And time untouched me with a trace
Of soul-smart or despair?

A WET AUGUST

Nine drops of water bead the jessamine,
And nine-and-ninety smear the stones and tiles:
—'Twas not so in that August—full-rayed, fine—
When we lived out-of-doors, sang songs, strode miles.

Or was there then no noted radiancy
Of summer? Were dun clouds, a dribbling bough,
Gilt over by the light I bore in me,
And was the waste world just the same as now?

It can have been so: yea, that threatenings
Of coming down-drip on the sunless gray,
By the then possibilities in things
Were wrought more bright than brightest skies to-day.

1920

THE DISSEMBLERS

"It was not you I came to please,
Only myself," flipped she;
"I like this spot of phantasies,
And thought you far from me."
But O, he was the secret spell
That led her to the lea!

"It was not she who shaped my ways,
Or works, or thoughts," he said.
"I scarcely marked her living days,
Or missed her much when dead."
But O, his joyance knew its knell
When daisies hid her head!

TO A LADY PLAYING AND SINGING IN THE MORNING

Joyful lady, sing!
And I will lurk here listening,
Though nought be done, and nought begun,
And work-hours swift are scurrying.

Sing, O lady, still!
Aye, I will wait each note you trill,
Though duties due that press to do
This whole day long I unfulfil.

"—It is an evening tune;
One not designed to waste the noon,"
You say. I know: time bids me go—
For daytide passes too, too soon!

But let indulgence be,
This once, to my rash ecstasy:

When sounds nowhere that carolled air
My idled morn may comfort me!

"A MAN WAS DRAWING NEAR TO ME"

On that gray night of mournful drone,
A part from aught to hear, to see,
I dreamt not that from shires unknown
In gloom, alone,
By Halworthy,
A man was drawing near to me.

I'd no concern at anything,
No sense of coming pull-heart play;
Yet, under the silent outspreading
Of even's wing
Where Otterham lay,
A man was riding up my way.

I thought of nobody—not of one,
But only of trifles—legends, ghosts—
Though, on the moorland dim and dun
That travellers shun
About these coasts,
The man had passed Tresparret Posts.

There was no light at all inland,
Only the seaward pharos-fire,
Nothing to let me understand
That hard at hand
By Hennett Byre
The man was getting nigh and nigher.

There was a rumble at the door,
A draught disturbed the drapery,
And but a minute passed before,
With gaze that bore
My destiny,
The man revealed himself to me.

THE STRANGE HOUSE

(MAX GATE, A.D. 2000)

"I hear the piano playing—
Just as a ghost might play."
"—O, but what are you saying?
There's no piano to-day;
Their old one was sold and broken;
Years past it went amiss."
"—I heard it, or shouldn't have spoken:
A strange house, this!

"I catch some undertone here,
From some one out of sight."
"—Impossible; we are alone here,
And shall be through the night."
"—The parlour-door—what stirred it?"
"—No one: no soul's in range."
"—But, anyhow, I heard it,
And it seems strange!

"Seek my own room I cannot—
A figure is on the stair!"
"—What figure? Nay, I scan not
Any one lingering there.
A bough outside is waving,
And that's its shade by the moon."
"—Well, all is strange! I am craving
Strength to leave soon."

"—Ah, maybe you've some vision
Of showings beyond our sphere;
Some sight, sense, intuition
Of what once happened here?
The house is old; they've hinted
It once held two love-thralls,
And they may have imprinted
Their dreams on its walls?

"They were—I think 'twas told me—
Queer in their works and ways;

The teller would often hold me
With weird tales of those days.
Some folk can not abide here,
But we—we do not care
Who loved, laughed, wept, or died here,
Knew joy, or despair."

"AS 'TWERE TO-NIGHT"

(SONG)

As 'twere to-night, in the brief space
Of a far eventime,
My spirit rang achime
At vision of a girl of grace;
As 'twere to-night, in the brief space
Of a far eventime.

As 'twere at noontide of to-morrow
I airily walked and talked,
And wondered as I walked
What it could mean, this soar from sorrow;
As 'twere at noontide of to-morrow
I airily walked and talked.

As 'twere at waning of this week
Broke a new life on me;
Trancings of bliss to be
In some dim dear land soon to seek;
As 'twere at waning of this week
Broke a new life on me!

THE CONTRETEMPS

A forward rush by the lamp in the gloom,
And we clasped, and almost kissed;
But she was not the woman whom
I had promised to meet in the thawing brume
On that harbour-bridge; nor was I he of her tryst.

So loosening from me swift she said:
"O why, why feign to be
The one I had meant!—to whom I have sped
To fly with, being so sorrily wed!"
—'Twas thus and thus that she upbraided me.

My assignation had struck upon
Some others' like it, I found.
And her lover rose on the night anon;
And then her husband entered on
The lamplit, snowflaked, sloppiness around.

"Take her and welcome, man!" he cried:
"I wash my hands of her.
I'll find me twice as good a bride!"
—All this to me, whom he had eyed,
Plainly, as his wife's planned deliverer.

And next the lover: "Little I knew,
Madam, you had a third!
Kissing here in my very view!"
—Husband and lover then withdrew.
I let them; and I told them not they erred.

Why not? Well, there faced she and I—
Two strangers who'd kissed, or near,
Chancewise. To see stand weeping by
A woman once embraced, will try
The tension of a man the most austere.

So it began; and I was young,
She pretty, by the lamp,
As flakes came waltzing down among

The waves of her clinging hair, that hung
Heavily on her temples, dark and damp.

And there alone still stood we two;
She one cast off for me,
Or so it seemed: while night ondrew,
Forcing a parley what should do
We twain hearts caught in one catastrophe.

In stranded souls a common strait
Wakes latencies unknown,
Whose impulse may precipitate
A life-long leap. The hour was late,
And there was the Jersey boat with its funnel agroan.

"Is wary walking worth much pother?"
It grunted, as still it stayed.
"One pairing is as good as another
Where all is venture! Take each other,
And scrap the oaths that you have aforetime made." . . .

—Of the four involved there walks but one
On earth at this late day.
And what of the chapter so begun?
In that odd complex what was done?
Well; happiness comes in full to none:
Let peace lie on lulled lips: I will not say.

Weymouth

A GENTLEMAN'S EPITAPH ON HIMSELF AND A LADY, WHO WERE BURIED TOGETHER

I dwelt in the shade of a city,
She far by the sea,
With folk perhaps good, gracious, witty;
But never with me.

23

Her form on the ballroom's smooth flooring
        I never once met,
To guide her with accents adoring
        Through Weippert's "First Set."[1]

I spent my life's seasons with pale ones
        In Vanity Fair,
And she enjoyed hers among hale ones
        In salt-smelling air.

Maybe she had eyes of deep colour,
        Maybe they were blue,
Maybe as she aged they got duller;
        That never I knew.

She may have had lips like the coral,
        But I never kissed them,
Saw pouting, nor curling in quarrel,
        Nor sought for, nor missed them.

Not a word passed of love all our lifetime,
        Between us, nor thrill;
We'd never a husband-and-wife time,
        For good or for ill.

Yet as one dust, through bleak days and vernal,
        Lie I and lies she,
This never-known lady, eternal
        Companion to me!

---

[1] Quadrilles danced early in the nineteenth century.

THE OLD GOWN

(SONG)

I have seen her in gowns the brightest,
    Of azure, green, and red,
And in the simplest, whitest,
    Muslined from heel to head;
I have watched her walking, riding,
    Shade-flecked by a leafy tree,
Or in fixed thought abiding
    By the foam-fingered sea.

In woodlands I have known her,
    When boughs were mourning loud,
In the rain-reek she has shown her
    Wild-haired and watery-browed.
And once or twice she has cast me
    As she pomped along the street
Court-clad, ere quite she had passed me,
    A glance from her chariot-seat.

But in my memoried passion
    For evermore stands she
In the gown of fading fashion
    She wore that night when we,
Doomed long to part, assembled
    In the snug small room; yea, when
She sang with lips that trembled,
    "Shall I see his face again?"

A NIGHT IN NOVEMBER

I marked when the weather changed,
And the panes began to quake,
And the winds rose up and ranged,
That night, lying half-awake.

25

Dead leaves blew into my room,
And alighted upon my bed,
And a tree declared to the gloom
Its sorrow that they were shed.

One leaf of them touched my hand,
And I thought that it was you
There stood as you used to stand,
And saying at last you knew!

(?) 1913

A DUETTIST TO HER PIANOFORTE

SONG OF SILENCE

(E. L. H.—H. C. H.)

Since every sound moves memories,
    How can I play you
Just as I might if you raised no scene,
By your ivory rows, of a form between
My vision and your time-worn sheen,
    As when each day you
Answered our fingers with ecstasy?
So it's hushed, hushed, hushed, you are for me!

And as I am doomed to counterchord
    Her notes no more
In those old things I used to know,
In a fashion, when we practised so,
"Good-night!—Good-bye!" to your pleated show
    Of silk, now hoar,
Each nodding hammer, and pedal and key,
For dead, dead, dead, you are to me!

I fain would second her, strike to her stroke,
    As when she was by,

26

Aye, even from the ancient clamorous "Fall
Of Paris," or "Battle of Prague" withal,
To the "Roving Minstrels," or "Elfin Call"
    Sung soft as a sigh:
But upping ghosts press achefully,
And mute, mute, mute, you are for me!
Should I fling your polyphones, plaints, and quavers
    Afresh on the air,
Too quick would the small white shapes be here
Of the fellow twain of hands so dear;
And a black-tressed profile, and pale smooth ear;
    —Then how shall I bear
Such heavily-haunted harmony?
Nay: hushed, hushed, hushed you are for me!

"WHERE THREE ROADS JOINED"

Where three roads joined it was green and fair,
And over a gate was the sun-glazed sea,
And life laughed sweet when I halted there;
Yet there I never again would be.

I am sure those branchways are brooding now,
With a wistful blankness upon their face,
While the few mute passengers notice how
Spectre-beridden is the place;

Which nightly sighs like a laden soul,
And grieves that a pair, in bliss for a spell
Not far from thence, should have let it roll
Away from them down a plumbless well

While the phasm of him who fared starts up,
And of her who was waiting him sobs from near,
As they haunt there and drink the wormwood cup
They filled for themselves when their sky was clear.

Yes, I see those roads—now rutted and bare,

27

While over the gate is no sun-glazed sea;
And though life laughed when I halted there,
It is where I never again would be.

"AND THERE WAS A GREAT CALM"

(ON THE SIGNING OF THE ARMISTICE, Nov. 11, 1918)

I

There had been years of Passion—scorching, cold,
And much Despair, and Anger heaving high,
Care whitely watching, Sorrows manifold,
Among the young, among the weak and old,
And the pensive Spirit of Pity whispered, "Why?"

II

Men had not paused to answer. Foes distraught
Pierced the thinned peoples in a brute-like blindness,
Philosophies that sages long had taught,
And Selflessness, were as an unknown thought,
And "Hell!" and "Shell!" were yapped at Lovingkindness.

III

The feeble folk at home had grown full-used
To "dug-outs," "snipers," "Huns," from the war-adept
In the mornings heard, and at evetides perused;
To day—dreamt men in millions, when they mused—
To nightmare-men in millions when they slept.

IV

Waking to wish existence timeless, null,
Sirius they watched above where armies fell;
He seemed to check his flapping when, in the lull

28

Of night a boom came thencewise, like the dull
Plunge of a stone dropped into some deep well.

V

So, when old hopes that earth was bettering slowly
Were dead and damned, there sounded "War is done!"
One morrow. Said the bereft, and meek, and lowly,
"Will men some day be given to grace? yea, wholly,
And in good sooth, as our dreams used to run?"

VI

Breathless they paused. Out there men raised their glance
To where had stood those poplars lank and lopped,
As they had raised it through the four years' dance
Of Death in the now familiar flats of France;
And murmured, "Strange, this! How? All firing stopped?"

VII

Aye; all was hushed. The about-to-fire fired not,
The aimed-at moved away in trance-lipped song.
One checkless regiment slung a clinching shot
And turned. The Spirit of Irony smirked out, "What?
Spoil peradventures woven of Rage and Wrong?"

VIII

Thenceforth no flying fires inflamed the gray,
No hurtlings shook the dewdrop from the thorn,
No moan perplexed the mute bird on the spray;
Worn horses mused: "We are not whipped to-day";
No weft-winged engines blurred the moon's thin horn.

IX

Calm fell. From Heaven distilled a clemency;
There was peace on earth, and silence in the sky;
Some could, some could not, shake off misery:
The Sinister Spirit sneered: "It had to be!"
And again the Spirit of Pity whispered, "Why?"

HAUNTING FINGERS

A PHANTASY IN A MUSEUM OF MUSICAL INSTRUMENTS

"Are you awake,
Comrades, this silent night?
Well 'twere if all of our glossy gluey make
Lay in the damp without, and fell to fragments quite!"

"O viol, my friend,
I watch, though Phosphor nears,
And I fain would drowse away to its utter end
This dumb dark stowage after our loud melodious years!"

And they felt past handlers clutch them,
Though none was in the room,
Old players' dead fingers touch them,
Shrunk in the tomb.

"'Cello, good mate,
You speak my mind as yours:
Doomed to this voiceless, crippled, corpselike state,
Who, dear to famed Amphion, trapped here, long endures?"

"Once I could thrill
The populace through and through,
Wake them to passioned pulsings past their will." . . .
(A contra-basso spake so, and the rest sighed anew.)

And they felt old muscles travel
Over their tense contours,
And with long skill unravel
Cunningest scores.

"The tender pat
Of her aery finger-tips
Upon me daily—I rejoiced thereat!"
(Thuswise a harpsicord, as from dampered lips.)

"My keys' white shine,
Now sallow, met a hand

30

Even whiter.... Tones of hers fell forth with mine
In sowings of sound so sweet no lover could withstand!"

And its clavier was filmed with fingers
Like tapering flames—wan, cold—
Or the nebulous light that lingers
In charnel mould.

"Gayer than most
Was I," reverbed a drum;
"The regiments, marchings, throngs, hurrahs! What a host
I stirred—even when crape mufflings gagged me well-nigh dumb!"

Trilled an aged viol:
"Much tune have I set free
To spur the dance, since my first timid trial
Where I had birth—far hence, in sun-swept Italy!"

And he feels apt touches on him
From those that pressed him then;
Who seem with their glance to con him,
Saying, "Not again!"

"A holy calm,"
Mourned a shawm's voice subdued,
"Steeped my Cecilian rhythms when hymn and psalm
Poured from devout souls met in Sabbath sanctitude."

"I faced the sock
Nightly," twanged a sick lyre,
"Over ranked lights! O charm of life in mock,
O scenes that fed love, hope, wit, rapture, mirth, desire!"

Thus they, till each past player
Stroked thinner and more thin,
And the morning sky grew grayer
And day crawled in.

THE WOMAN I MET

A stranger, I threaded sunken-hearted
   A lamp-lit crowd;
And anon there passed me a soul departed,
   Who mutely bowed.
In my far-off youthful years I had met her,
Full-pulsed; but now, no more life's debtor,
   Onward she slid
  In a shroud that furs half-hid.

"Why do you trouble me, dead woman,
   Trouble me;
You whom I knew when warm and human?
   —How it be
That you quitted earth and are yet upon it
Is, to any who ponder on it,
   Past being read!"
  "Still, it is so," she said.

"These were my haunts in my olden sprightly
   Hours of breath;
Here I went tempting frail youth nightly
   To their death;
But you deemed me chaste—me, a tinselled sinner!
How thought you one with pureness in her
   Could pace this street
  Eyeing some man to greet?

"Well; your very simplicity made me love you
   Mid such town dross,
Till I set not Heaven itself above you,
   Who grew my Cross;
For you'd only nod, despite how I sighed for you;
So you tortured me, who fain would have died for you!
   —What I suffered then
  Would have paid for the sins of ten!

"Thus went the days. I feared you despised me
   To fling me a nod
Each time, no more: till love chastised me
   As with a rod

That a fresh bland boy of no assurance
Should fire me with passion beyond endurance,
    While others all
  I hated, and loathed their call.

"I said: 'It is his mother's spirit
    Hovering around
To shield him, maybe!' I used to fear it,
    As still I found
My beauty left no least impression,
And remnants of pride withheld confession
    Of my true trade
  By speaking; so I delayed.

"I said: 'Perhaps with a costly flower
    He'll be beguiled.'
I held it, in passing you one late hour,
    To your face: you smiled,
Keeping step with the throng; though you did not see
there
A single one that rivalled me there! . . .
    Well: it's all past.
  I died in the Lock at last."

So walked the dead and I together
    The quick among,
Elbowing our kind of every feather
    Slowly and long;
Yea, long and slowly. That a phantom should stalk there
With me seemed nothing strange, and talk there
    That winter night
  By flaming jets of light.

She showed me Juans who feared their call-time,
    Guessing their lot;
She showed me her sort that cursed their fall-time,
    And that did not.
Till suddenly murmured she: "Now, tell me,
Why asked you never, ere death befell me,
    To have my love,
  Much as I dreamt thereof?"

I could not answer. And she, well weeting
    All in my heart,

Said: "God your guardian kept our fleeting
   Forms apart!"
Sighing and drawing her furs around her
Over the shroud that tightly bound her,
   With wafts as from clay
  She turned and thinned away.

London, 1918

"IF IT'S EVER SPRING AGAIN"

(SONG)

If it's ever spring again,
  Spring again,
I shall go where went I when
Down the moor-cock splashed, and hen,
Seeing me not, amid their flounder,
Standing with my arm around her;
If it's ever spring again,
  Spring again,
I shall go where went I then.

If it's ever summer-time,
  Summer-time,
With the hay crop at the prime,
And the cuckoos—two—in rhyme,
As they used to be, or seemed to,
We shall do as long we've dreamed to,
If it's ever summer-time,
  Summer-time,
With the hay, and bees achime.

THE TWO HOUSES

In the heart of night,
When farers were not near,
The left house said to the house on the right,
"I have marked your rise, O smart newcomer here."

Said the right, cold-eyed:
"Newcomer here I am,
Hence haler than you with your cracked old hide,
Loose casements, wormy beams, and doors that jam.

"Modern my wood,
My hangings fair of hue;
While my windows open as they should,
And water-pipes thread all my chambers through.

"Your gear is gray,
Your face wears furrows untold."
"—Yours might," mourned the other, "if you held, brother,
The Presences from aforetime that I hold.

"You have not known
Men's lives, deaths, toils, and teens;
You are but a heap of stick and stone:
A new house has no sense of the have-beens.

"Void as a drum
You stand: I am packed with these,
Though, strangely, living dwellers who come
See not the phantoms all my substance sees!

"Visible in the morning
Stand thcy, when dawn drags in;
Visible at night; yet hint or warning
Of these thin elbowers few of the inmates win.

"Babes new-brought-forth
Obsess my rooms; straight-stretched
Lank corpses, ere outborne to earth;
Yea, throng they as when first from the 'Byss upfetched.

35

"Dancers and singers
Throb in me now as once;
Rich-noted throats and gossamered fingers
Of heels; the learned in love-lore and the dunce.

"Note here within
The bridegroom and the bride,
Who smile and greet their friends and kin,
And down my stairs depart for tracks untried.

"Where such inbe,
A dwelling's character
Takes theirs, and a vague semblancy
To them in all its limbs, and light, and atmosphere.

"Yet the blind folk
My tenants, who come and go
In the flesh mid these, with souls unwoke,
Of such sylph-like surrounders do not know."

"—Will the day come,"
Said the new one, awestruck, faint,
"When I shall lodge shades dim and dumb—
And with such spectral guests become acquaint?"

"—That will it, boy;
Such shades will people thee,
Each in his misery, irk, or joy,
And print on thee their presences as on me."

ON STINSFORD HILL AT MIDNIGHT

I glimpsed a woman's muslined form
Sing-songing airily
Against the moon; and still she sang,
And took no heed of me.

Another trice, and I beheld
What first I had not scanned,

That now and then she tapped and shook
A timbrel in her hand.

So late the hour, so white her drape,
So strange the look it lent
To that blank hill, I could not guess
What phantastry it meant.

Then burst I forth: "Why such from you?
Are you so happy now?"
Her voice swam on; nor did she show
Thought of me anyhow.

I called again: "Come nearer; much
That kind of note I need!"
The song kept softening, loudening on,
In placid calm unheed.

"What home is yours now?" then I said;
"You seem to have no care."
But the wild wavering tune went forth
As if I had not been there.

"This world is dark, and where you are,"
I said, "I cannot be!"
But still the happy one sang on,
And had no heed of me.

THE FALLOW DEER AT THE LONELY HOUSE

One without looks in to-night
Through the curtain-chink
From the sheet of glistening white;
One without looks in to-night
As we sit and think
By the fender-brink.

37

We do not discern those eyes
Watching in the snow;
Lit by lamps of rosy dyes
We do not discern those eyes
Wondering, aglow,
Fourfooted, tiptoe.

THE SELFSAME SONG

A bird bills the selfsame song,
With never a fault in its flow,
That we listened to here those long
　　Long years ago.

A pleasing marvel is how
A strain of such rapturous rote
Should have gone on thus till now
　　Unchanged in a note!

—But it's not the selfsame bird.—
No: perished to dust is he . . .
As also are those who heard
　　That song with me.

THE WANDERER

There is nobody on the road
But I,
And no beseeming abode
I can try
For shelter, so abroad
I must lie.

The stars feel not far up,
And to be
The lights by which I sup
Glimmeringly,
Set out in a hollow cup
Over me.

They wag as though they were
Panting for joy
Where they shine, above all care,
And annoy,
And demons of despair—
Life's alloy.

Sometimes outside the fence
Feet swing past,
Clock-like, and then go hence,
Till at last
There is a silence, dense,
Deep, and vast.

A wanderer, witch-drawn
To and fro,
To-morrow, at the dawn,
On I go,
And where I rest anon
Do not know!

Yct it's meet—this bed of hay
And roofless plight;
For there's a house of clay,
My own, quite,
To roof me soon, all day
And all night.

A WIFE COMES BACK

This is the story a man told me
Of his life's one day of dreamery.

A woman came into his room
Between the dawn and the creeping day:
She was the years-wed wife from whom
He had parted, and who lived far away,
    As if strangers they.

He wondered, and as she stood
She put on youth in her look and air,
And more was he wonderstruck as he viewed
Her form and flesh bloom yet more fair
    While he watched her there;

Till she freshed to the pink and brown
That were hers on the night when first they met,
When she was the charm of the idle town
And he the pick of the club-fire set . . .
    His eyes grew wet,

And he stretched his arms: "Stay—rest!—"
He cried. "Abide with me so, my own!"
But his arms closed in on his hard bare breast;
She had vanished with all he had looked upon
    Of her beauty: gone.

He clothed, and drew downstairs,
But she was not in the house, he found;
And he passed out under the leafy pairs
Of the avenue elms, and searched around
    To the park-pale bound.

He mounted, and rode till night
To the city to which she had long withdrawn,
The vision he bore all day in his sight
Being her young self as pondered on
    In the dim of dawn.

"—The lady here long ago—

Is she now here?—young—or such age as she is?"
"—She is still here."—"Thank God. Let her know;
 She'll pardon a comer so late as this
     Whom she'd fain not miss."

 She received him—an ancient dame,
Who hemmed, with features frozen and numb,
"How strange!—I'd almost forgotten your name!—
     A call just now—is troublesome;
        Why did you come?"

A YOUNG MAN'S EXHORTATION

   Call off your eyes from care
By some determined deftness; put forth joys
Dear as excess without the core that cloys,
   And charm Life's lourings fair.

   Exalt and crown the hour
That girdles us, and fill it full with glee,
Blind glee, excelling aught could ever be
   Were heedfulness in power.

   Send up such touching strains
That limitless recruits from Fancy's pack
Shall rush upon your tongue, and tender back
   All that your soul contains.

   For what do we know best?
That a fresh love-leaf crumpled soon will dry,
And that men moment after moment die,
   Of all scope dispossest.

If I have seen one thing
It is the passing preciousness of dreams;
That aspects are within us; and who seems
   Most kingly is the King.

1867: Westbourne Park Villas.

41

AT LULWORTH COVE A CENTURY BACK

Had I but lived a hundred years ago
I might have gone, as I have gone this year,
By Warmwell Cross on to a Cove I know,
And Time have placed his finger on me there:

"You see that man?"—I might have looked, and said,
"O yes: I see him. One that boat has brought
Which dropped down Channel round Saint Alban's Head.
So commonplace a youth calls not my thought."

"You see that man?"—"Why yes; I told you; yes:
Of an idling town-sort; thin; hair brown in hue;
And as the evening light scants less and less
He looks up at a star, as many do."

"You see that man?"—"Nay, leave me!" then I plead,
"I have fifteen miles to vamp across the lea,
And it grows dark, and I am weary-kneed:
I have said the third time; yes, that man I see!

"Good. That man goes to Rome—to death, despair;
And no one notes him now but you and I:
A hundred years, and the world will follow him there,
And bend with reverence where his ashes lie."

September 1920

Note.—In September 1820 Keats, on his way to Rome, landed one day on the Dorset coast, and composed the sonnet, "Bright star! would I were steadfast as thou art." The spot of his landing is judged to have been Lulworth Cove.

A BYGONE OCCASION

(SONG)

That night, that night,
That song, that song!
Will such again be evened quite
Through lifetimes long?

No mirth was shown
To outer seers,
But mood to match has not been known
In modern years.

O eyes that smiled,
O lips that lured;
That such would last was one beguiled
To think ensured!

That night, that night,
That song, that song;
O drink to its recalled delight,
Though tears may throng!

TWO SERENADES

I

On Christmas Eve

Late on Christmas Eve, in the street alone,
Outside a house, on the pavement-stone,
I sang to her, as we'd sung together
On former eves ere I felt her tether.—
Above the door of green by me
Was she, her casement seen by me;
But she would not heed
What I melodied

In my soul's sore need—
She would not heed.

Cassiopeia overhead,
And the Seven of the Wain, heard what I said
As I bent me there, and voiced, and fingered
Upon the strings. . . . Long, long I lingered:
Only the curtains hid from her
One whom caprice had bid from her;
But she did not come,
And my heart grew numb
And dull my strum;
She did not come.

II

A Year Later

I skimmed the strings; I sang quite low;
I hoped she would not come or know
That the house next door was the one now dittied,
Not hers, as when I had played unpitied;
—Next door, where dwelt a heart fresh stirred,
My new Love, of good will to me,
Unlike my old Love chill to me,
Who had not cared for my notes when heard:
Yet that old Love came
To the other's name
As hers were the claim;
Yea, the old Love came

My viol sank mute, my tongue stood still,
I tried to sing on, but vain my will:
I prayed she would guess of the later, and leave me;
She stayed, as though, were she slain by the smart,
She would bear love's burn for a newer heart.
The tense-drawn moment wrought to bereave me
Of voice, and I turned in a dumb despair
At her finding I'd come to another there.
Sick I withdrew
At love's grim hue
Ere my last Love knew;
Sick I withdrew.

From an old copy.

44

THE WEDDING MORNING

Tabitha dressed for her wedding:—
"Tabby, why look so sad?"
"—O I feel a great gloominess spreading, spreading,
Instead of supremely glad! . . .

"I called on Carry last night,
And he came whilst I was there,
Not knowing I'd called. So I kept out of sight,
And I heard what he said to her:

"'—Ah, I'd far liefer marry
You, Dear, to-morrow!' he said,
'But that cannot be.'—O I'd give him to Carry,
And willingly see them wed,

"But how can I do it when
His baby will soon be born?
After that I hope I may die. And then
She can have him. I shall not mourn!"

END OF THE YEAR 1912

You were here at his young beginning,
You are not here at his agèd end;
Off he coaxed you from Life's mad spinning,
Lest you should see his form extend
Shivering, sighing,
Slowly dying,
And a tear on him expend.

So it comes that we stand lonely
In the star-lit avenue,
Dropping broken lipwords only,
For we hear no songs from you,
Such as flew here

45

For the new year
Once, while six bells swung thereto.

THE CHIMES PLAY "LIFE'S A BUMPER!"

"Awake! I'm off to cities far away,"
I said; and rose, on peradventures bent.
The chimes played "Life's a Bumper!" on that day
To the measure of my walking as I went:
Their sweetness frisked and floated on the lea,
As they played out "Life's a Bumper!" there to me.

"Awake!" I said. "I go to take a bride!"
—The sun arose behind me ruby-red
As I journeyed townwards from the countryside,
The chiming bells saluting near ahead.
Their sweetness swelled in tripping tings of glee
As they played out "Life's a Bumper!" there to me.

 "Again arise." I seek a turfy slope,
And go forth slowly on an autumn noon,
And there I lay her who has been my hope,
And think, "O may I follow hither soon!"
While on the wind the chimes come cheerily,
Playing out "Life's a Bumper!" there to me.

1913

"I WORKED NO WILE TO MEET YOU"

(SONG)

I worked no wile to meet you,
  My sight was set elsewhere,
I sheered about to shun you,
  And lent your life no care.
I was unprimed to greet you
  At such a date and place,
Constraint alone had won you
  Vision of my strange face!

You did not seek to see me
  Then or at all, you said,
—Meant passing when you neared me,
  But stumblingblocks forbade.
You even had thought to flee me,
  By other mindings moved;
No influent star endeared me,
  Unknown, unrecked, unproved!

What, then, was there to tell us
  The flux of flustering hours
Of their own tide would bring us
  By no device of ours
To where the daysprings well us
  Heart-hydromels that cheer,
Till Time enearth and swing us
  Round with the turning sphere.

AT THE RAILWAY STATION, UPWAY

"There is not much that I can do,
For I've no money that's quite my own!"
  Spoke up the pitying child—
A little boy with a violin

47

At the station before the train came in,—
"But I can play my fiddle to you,
And a nice one 'tis, and good in tone!"

  The man in the handcuffs smiled;
The constable looked, and he smiled, too,
  As the fiddle began to twang;
And the man in the handcuffs suddenly sang
    Uproariously:
    "This life so free
    Is the thing for me!"
And the constable smiled, and said no word,
As if unconscious of what he heard;
And so they went on till the train came in—
The convict, and boy with the violin.

SIDE BY SIDE

So there sat they,
The estranged two,
Thrust in one pew
By chance that day;
Placed so, breath-nigh,
Each comer unwitting
Who was to be sitting
In touch close by.

Thus side by side
Blindly alighted,
They seemed united
As groom and bride,
Who'd not communed
For many years—
Lives from twain spheres
With hearts distuned.

Her fringes brushed
His garment's hem

As the harmonies rushed
Through each of them:
Her lips could be heard
In the creed and psalms,
And their fingers neared
At the giving of alms.

And women and men,
The matins ended,
By looks commended
Them, joined again.
Quickly said she,
"Don't undeceive them—
Better thus leave them:"
"Quite so," said he.

Slight words!—the last
Between them said,
Those two, once wed,
Who had not stood fast.
Diverse their ways
From the western door,
To meet no more
In their span of days.

DREAM OF THE CITY SHOPWOMAN

'Twere sweet to have a comrade here,
Who'd vow to love this garreteer,
By city people's snap and sneer
    Tried oft and hard!

We'd rove a truant cock and hen
To some snug solitary glen,
And never be seen to haunt again
    This teeming yard.

Within a cot of thatch and clay

We'd list the flitting pipers play,
Our lives a twine of good and gay
    Enwreathed discreetly;

Our blithest deeds so neighbouring wise
That doves should coo in soft surprise,
"These must belong to Paradise
    Who live so sweetly."

Our clock should be the closing flowers,
Our sprinkle-bath the passing showers,
Our church the alleyed willow bowers,
    The truth our theme;

And infant shapes might soon abound:
Their shining heads would dot us round
Like mushroom balls on grassy ground . . .
    —But all is dream!

O God, that creatures framed to feel
A yearning nature's strong appeal
Should writhe on this eternal wheel
    In rayless grime;

And vainly note, with wan regret,
Each star of early promise set;
Till Death relieves, and they forget
    Their one Life's time!

Westbourne Park Villas, 1866

A MAIDEN'S PLEDGE

(SONG)

I do not wish to win your vow
To take me soon or late as bride,
And lift me from the nook where now

I tarry your farings to my side.
I am blissful ever to abide
In this green labyrinth—let all be,
If but, whatever may betide,
You do not leave off loving me!

Your comet-comings I will wait
With patience time shall not wear through;
The yellowing years will not abate
My largened love and truth to you,
Nor drive me to complaint undue
Of absence, much as I may pine,
If never another 'twixt us two
Shall come, and you stand wholly mine.

THE CHILD AND THE SAGE

You say, O Sage, when weather-checked,
        "I have been favoured so
    With cloudless skies, I must expect
        This dash of rain or snow."

"Since health has been my lot," you say,
        "So many months of late,
    I must not chafe that one short day
        Of sickness mars my state."

You say, "Such bliss has been my share
        From Love's unbroken smile,
    It is but reason I should bear
        A cross therein awhile."

And thus you do not count upon
        Continuance of joy;
    But, when at ease, expect anon
        A burden of annoy.

But, Sage—this Earth—why not a place

Where no reprisals reign,
Where never a spell of pleasantness
Makes reasonable a pain?

December 21, 1908

MISMET

I

He was leaning by a face,
He was looking into eyes,
And he knew a trysting-place,
And he heard seductive sighs;
   But the face,
   And the eyes,
   And the place,
   And the sighs,
Were not, alas, the right ones—the ones meet for him—
Though fine and sweet the features, and the feelings all
abrim.

II

She was looking at a form,
She was listening for a tread,
She could feel a waft of charm
When a certain name was said;
   But the form,
   And the tread,
   And the charm
   Of name said,
Were the wrong ones for her, and ever would be so,
While the heritor of the right it would have saved her
soul to know!

AN AUTUMN RAIN-SCENE

There trudges one to a merry-making
With a sturdy swing,
On whom the rain comes down.

To fetch the saving medicament
Is another bent,
On whom the rain comes down.

One slowly drives his herd to the stall
Ere ill befall,
On whom the rain comes down.

This bears his missives of life and death
With quickening breath,
On whom the rain comes down.

One watches for signals of wreck or war
From the hill afar,
On whom the rain comes down.

No care if he gain a shelter or none,
Unhired moves one,
On whom the rain comes down.

And another knows nought of its chilling fall
Upon him at all,
On whom the rain comes down.

October 1904

MEDITATIONS ON A HOLIDAY

(A NEW THEME TO AN OLD FOLK-JINGLE)

'Tis May morning,
All-adorning,

No cloud warning
  Of rain to-day.
Where shall I go to,
Go to, go to?—
Can I say No to
  Lyonnesse-way?

Well—what reason
Now at this season
Is there for treason
  To other shrines?
Tristram is not there,
Isolt forgot there,
New eras blot there
  Sought-for signs!

Stratford-on-Avon—
Poesy-paven—
I'll find a haven
  There, somehow!—
Nay—I'm but caught of
Dreams long thought of,
The Swan knows nought of
  His Avon now!

What shall it be, then,
I go to see, then,
Under the plea, then,
  Of votary?
I'll go to Lakeland,
Lakeland, Lakeland,
Certainly Lakeland
  Let it be.

But—why to that place,
That place, that place,
Such a hard come-at place
  Need I fare?
When its bard cheers no more,
Loves no more, fears no more,
Sees no more, hears no more
  Anything there!

Ah, there is Scotland,

Burns's Scotland,
And Waverley's. To what land
    Better can I hie?—
Yet—if no whit now
Feel those of it now—
Care not a bit now
    For it—why I?

I'll seek a town street,
Aye, a brick-brown street,
Quite a tumbledown street,
    Drawing no eyes.
For a Mary dwelt there,
And a Percy felt there
Heart of him melt there,
    A Claire likewise.

Why incline to that city,
Such a city, that city,
Now a mud-bespat city!—
    Care the lovers who
Now live and walk there,
Sit there and talk there,
Buy there, or hawk there,
    Or wed, or woo?

Laughters in a volley
Greet so fond a folly
As nursing melancholy
    In this and that spot,
Which, with most endeavour,
Those can visit never,
But for ever and ever
    Will now know not!

If, on lawns Elysian,
With a broadened vision
And a faint derision
    Conscious be they,
How they might reprove me
That these fancies move me,
Think they ill behoove me,
    Smile, and say:

"What!—our hoar old houses,
Where the past dead-drowses,
Nor a child nor spouse is
    Of our name at all?
Such abodes to care for,
Inquire about and bear for,
And suffer wear and tear for—
    How weak of you and small!"

May 1921

AN EXPERIENCE

Wit, weight, or wealth there was not
    In anything that was said,
    In anything that was done;
All was of scope to cause not
    A triumph, dazzle, or dread
    To even the subtlest one,
        My friend,
    To even the subtlest one.

But there was a new afflation—
    An aura zephyring round,
    That care infected not:
It came as a salutation,
    And, in my sweet astound,
    I scarcely witted what
        Might pend,
    I scarcely witted what.

The hills in samewise to me
    Spoke, as they grayly gazed,
    —First hills to speak so yet!
The thin-edged breezes blew me
    What I, though cobwebbed, crazed,
    Was never to forget,
        My friend,
    Was never to forget!

56

THE BEAUTY

O do not praise my beauty more,
  In such word-wild degree,
And say I am one all eyes adore;
  For these things harass me!

But do for ever softly say:
  "From now unto the end
Come weal, come wanzing, come what may,
  Dear, I will be your friend."

I hate my beauty in the glass:
  My beauty is not I:
I wear it: none cares whether, alas,
  Its wearer live or die!

The inner I O care for, then,
  Yea, me and what I am,
And shall be at the gray hour when
  My cheek begins to clam.

Note.—"The Regent Street beauty, Miss Verrey, the Swiss confectioner's daughter, whose personal attractions have been so mischievously exaggerated, died of fever on Monday evening, brought on by the annoyance she had been for some time subject to."—London paper, October 1828.

THE COLLECTOR CLEANS HIS PICTURE

Fili hominis, ecce ego tollo a te desiderabile oculorum tuorom in plaga.—Ezech. xxiv. 16.

How I remember cleaning that strange picture!
I had been deep in duty for my sick neighbour—
His besides my own—over several Sundays,
Often, too, in the week; so with parish pressures,

57

Baptisms, burials, doctorings, conjugal counsel—
All the whatnots asked of a rural parson—
Faith, I was well-nigh broken, should have been fully
Saving for one small secret relaxation,
One that in mounting manhood had grown my hobby.

This was to delve at whiles for easel-lumber,
Stowed in the backmost slums of a soon-reached city,
Merely on chance to uncloak some worthy canvas,
Panel, or plaque, blacked blind by uncouth adventure,
Yet under all concealing a precious art-feat.
Such I had found not yet. My latest capture
Came from the rooms of a trader in ancient house-gear
Who had no scent of beauty or soul for brushcraft.
Only a tittle cost it—murked with grime-films,
Gatherings of slow years, thick-varnished over,
Never a feature manifest of man's painting.

So, one Saturday, time ticking hard on midnight
Ere an hour subserved, I set me upon it.
Long with coiled-up sleeves I cleaned and yet cleaned,
Till a first fresh spot, a high light, looked forth,
Then another, like fair flesh, and another;
Then a curve, a nostril, and next a finger,
Tapering, shapely, significantly pointing slantwise.
"Flemish?" I said. "Nay, Spanish . . . But, nay, Italian!"
—Then meseemed it the guise of the ranker Venus,
Named of some Astarte, of some Cotytto.
Down I knelt before it and kissed the panel,
Drunk with the lure of love's inhibited dreamings.

Till the dawn I rubbed, when there gazed up at me
A hag, that had slowly emerged from under my hands there,
Pointing the slanted finger towards a bosom
Eaten away of a rot from the lusts of a lifetime . . .
—I could have ended myself in heart-shook horror.
Stunned I sat till roused by a clear-voiced bell-chime,
Fresh and sweet as the dew-fleece under my luthern.
It was the matin service calling to me
From the adjacent steeple.

THE WOOD FIRE

(A FRAGMENT)

"This is a brightsome blaze you've lit good friend, to-night!"
"—Aye, it has been the bleakest spring I have felt for years,
And nought compares with cloven logs to keep alight:
I buy them bargain-cheap of the executioners,
As I dwell near; and they wanted the crosses out of sight
By Passover, not to affront the eyes of visitors.

"Yes, they're from the crucifixions last week-ending
At Kranion. We can sometimes use the poles again,
But they get split by the nails, and 'tis quicker work than mending
To knock together new; though the uprights now and then
Serve twice when they're let stand. But if a feast's impending,
As lately, you've to tidy up for the corners' ken.

"Though only three were impaled, you may know it didn't pass off
So quietly as was wont? That Galilee carpenter's son
Who boasted he was king, incensed the rabble to scoff:
I heard the noise from my garden. This piece is the one he was on . . .
Yes, it blazes up well if lit with a few dry chips and shroff;
And it's worthless for much else, what with cuts and stains thereon."

SAYING GOOD-BYE

(SONG)

We are always saying
"Good-bye, good-bye!"
In work, in playing,

59

In gloom, in gaying:
At many a stage
Of pilgrimage
From youth to age
We say, "Good-bye,
Good-bye!"

We are undiscerning
Which go to sigh,
Which will be yearning
For soon returning;
And which no more
Will dark our door,
Or tread our shore,
But go to die,
To die.

Some come from roaming
With joy again;
Some, who come homing
By stealth at gloaming,
Had better have stopped
Till death, and dropped
By strange hands propped,
Than come so fain,
So fain.

So, with this saying,
"Good-bye, good-bye,"
We speed their waying
Without betraying
Our grief, our fear
No more to hear
From them, close, clear,
Again: "Good-bye,
Good-bye!"

ON THE TUNE CALLED THE OLD-
HUNDRED-AND-FOURTH

We never sang together
   Ravenscroft's terse old tune
On Sundays or on weekdays,
In sharp or summer weather,
   At night-time or at noon.

Why did we never sing it,
   Why never so incline
On Sundays or on weekdays,
Even when soft wafts would wing it
   From your far floor to mine?

Shall we that tune, then, never
   Stand voicing side by side
On Sundays or on weekdays? . . .
Or shall we, when for ever
   In Sheol we abide,

Sing it in desolation,
   As we might long have done
On Sundays or on weekdays
With love and exultation
   Before our sands had run?

THE OPPORTUNITY

(FOR H. P.)

Forty springs back, I recall,
We met at this phase of the Maytime:
We might have clung close through all,
But we parted when died that daytime.

We parted with smallest regret;

61

Perhaps should have cared but slightly,
Just then, if we never had met:
Strange, strange that we lived so lightly!

Had we mused a little space
At that critical date in the Maytime,
One life had been ours, one place,
Perhaps, till our long cold daytime.

—This is a bitter thing
For thee, O man: what ails it?
The tide of chance may bring
Its offer; but nought avails it!

EVELYN G. OF CHRISTMINSTER

I can see the towers
In mind quite clear
Not many hours'
Faring from here;
But how up and go,
And briskly bear
Thither, and know
That are not there?

Though the birds sing small,
And apple and pear
On your trees by the wall
Are ripe and rare,
Though none excel them,
I have no care
To taste them or smell them
And you not there.

Though the College stones
Are smit with the sun,
And the graduates and Dons
Who held you as one

Of brightest brow
Still think as they did,
Why haunt with them now
Your candle is hid?

Towards the river
A pealing swells:
They cost me a quiver—
Those prayerful bells!
How go to God,
Who can reprove
With so heavy a rod
As your swift remove!

The chorded keys
Wait all in a row,
And the bellows wheeze
As long ago.
And the psalter lingers,
And organist's chair;
But where are your fingers
That once wagged there?

Shall I then seek
That desert place
This or next week,
And those tracks trace
That fill me with cark
And cloy; nowhere
Being movement or mark
Of you now there!

THE RIFT

(Song: Minor Mode)

'Twas just at gnat and cobweb-time,
When yellow begins to show in the leaf,

That your old gamut changed its chime
From those true tones—of span so brief!—
That met my beats of joy, of grief,
  As rhyme meets rhyme.

So sank I from my high sublime!
We faced but chancewise after that,
And never I knew or guessed my crime. . .
Yes; 'twas the date—or nigh thereat—
Of the yellowing leaf; at moth and gnat
  And cobweb-time.

VOICES FROM THINGS GROWING IN A
CHURCHYARD

These flowers are I, poor Fanny Hurd,
  Sir or Madam,
A little girl here sepultured.
Once I flit-fluttered like a bird
Above the grass, as now I wave
In daisy shapes above my grave,
  All day cheerily,
  All night eerily!

—I am one Bachelor Bowring, "Gent,"
  Sir or Madam;
In shingled oak my bones were pent;
Hence more than a hundred years I spent
In my feat of change from a coffin-thrall
To a dancer in green as leaves on a wall.
  All day cheerily,
  All night eerily!

—I, these berries of juice and gloss,
  Sir or Madam,
Am clean forgotten as Thomas Voss;
Thin-urned, I have burrowed away from the moss
That covers my sod, and have entered this yew,

And turned to clusters ruddy of view,
    All day cheerily,
    All night eerily!

—The Lady Gertrude, proud, high-bred,
    Sir or Madam,
Am I—this laurel that shades your head;
Into its veins I have stilly sped,
And made them of me; and my leaves now shine,
As did my satins superfine,
    All day cheerily,
    All night eerily!

—I, who as innocent withwind climb,
    Sir or Madam.
Am one Eve Greensleeves, in olden time
Kissed by men from many a clime,
Beneath sun, stars, in blaze, in breeze,
As now by glowworms and by bees,
    All day cheerily,
    All night eerily![2]

—I'm old Squire Audeley Grey, who grew,
    Sir or Madam,
Aweary of life, and in scorn withdrew;
Till anon I clambered up anew
As ivy-green, when my ache was stayed,
And in that attire I have longtime gayed
    All day cheerily,
    All night eerily!

—And so they breathe, these masks, to each
    Sir or Madam
Who lingers there, and their lively speech
Affords an interpreter much to teach,
As their murmurous accents seem to come
Thence hitheraround in a radiant hum,
    All day cheerily,
    All night eerily!

---

[2] It was said her real name was Eve Trevillian or Trevelyan; and that she was the handsome mother of two or three illegitimate children, circa 1784–95.

ON THE WAY

The trees fret fitfully and twist,
Shutters rattle and carpets heave,
Slime is the dust of yestereve,
 And in the streaming mist
Fishes might seem to fin a passage if they list.

 But to his feet,
 Drawing nigh and nigher
 A hidden seat,
 The fog is sweet
 And the wind a lyre.

A vacant sameness grays the sky,
 A moisture gathers on each knop
Of the bramble, rounding to a drop,
 That greets the goer-by
With the cold listless lustre of a dead man's eye.

 But to her sight,
 Drawing nigh and nigher
 Its deep delight,
 The fog is bright
 And the wind a lyre.

"SHE DID NOT TURN"

 She did not turn,
But passed foot-faint with averted head
In her gown of green, by the bobbing fern,
Though I leaned over the gate that led
From where we waited with table spread;
 But she did not turn:
Why was she near there if love had fled?

 She did not turn,

Though the gate was whence I had often sped
In the mists of morning to meet her, and learn
Her heart, when its moving moods I read
As a book—she mine, as she sometimes said;
    But she did not turn,
And passed foot-faint with averted head.

GROWTH IN MAY

I enter a daisy-and-buttercup land,
  And thence thread a jungle of grass:
Hurdles and stiles scarce visible stand
  Above the lush stems as I pass.

Hedges peer over, and try to be seen,
  And seem to reveal a dim sense
That amid such ambitious and elbow-high green
  They make a mean show as a fence.

Elsewhere the mead is possessed of the neats,
  That range not greatly above
The rich rank thicket which brushes their teats,
  And her gown, as she waits for her Love.

Near Chard

THE CHILDREN AND SIR NAMELESS

Sir Nameless, once of Athelhall, declared:
"These wretched children romping in my park
Trample the herbage till the soil is bared,
And yap and yell from early morn till dark!
Go keep them harnessed to their set routines:

Thank God I've none to hasten my decay;
For green remembrance there are better means
Than offspring, who but wish their sires away."

Sir Nameless of that mansion said anon:
"To be perpetuate for my mightiness
Sculpture must image me when I am gone."
—He forthwith summoned carvers there express
To shape a figure stretching seven-odd feet
(For he was tall) in alabaster stone,
With shield, and crest, and casque, and word complete:
When done a statelier work was never known.

Three hundred years hied; Church-restorers came,
And, no one of his lineage being traced,
They thought an effigy so large in frame
Best fitted for the floor. There it was placed,
Under the seats for schoolchildren. And they
Kicked out his name, and hobnailed off his nose;
And, as they yawn through sermon-time, they say,
"Who was this old stone man beneath our toes?"

AT THE ROYAL ACADEMY

These summer landscapes—clump, and copse, and croft—
Woodland and meadowland—here hung aloft,
Gay with limp grass and leafery new and soft,

Seem caught from the immediate season's yield
I saw last noonday shining over the field,
By rapid snatch, while still are uncongealed

The saps that in their live originals climb;
Yester's quick greenage here set forth in mime
Just as it stands, now, at our breathing-time.

But these young foils so fresh upon each tree,
Soft verdures spread in sprouting novelty,
Are not this summer's, though they feign to be.

Last year their May to Michaelmas term was run,
Last autumn browned and buried every one,
And no more know they sight of any sun.

HER TEMPLE

Dear, think not that they will forget you:
  —If craftsmanly art should be mine
I will build up a temple, and set you
  Therein as its shrine.

They may say: "Why a woman such honour?"
  —Be told, "O, so sweet was her fame,
That a man heaped this splendour upon her;
  None now knows his name."

A TWO-YEARS' IDYLL

Yes; such it was;
Just those two seasons unsought,
Sweeping like summertide wind on our ways;
Moving, as straws,
Hearts quick as ours in those days;
Going like wind, too, and rated as nought
Save as the prelude to plays
Soon to come—larger, life-fraught:
Yes; such it was.

"Nought" it was called,
Even by ourselves—that which springs
Out of the years for all flesh, first or last,
Commonplace, scrawled
Dully on days that go past.

Yet, all the while, it upbore us like wings
Even in hours overcast:
Aye, though this best thing of things,
"Nought" it was called!

What seems it now?
Lost: such beginning was all;
Nothing came after: romance straight forsook
Quickly somehow
Life when we sped from our nook,
Primed for new scenes with designs smart and tall . . .
—A preface without any book,
A trumpet uplipped, but no call;
That seems it now.

BY HENSTRIDGE CROSS AT THE YEAR'S END

(From this centuries-old cross-road the highway leads east to
London, north to Bristol and Bath, west to Exeter and the Land's
End, and south to the Channel coast.)

Why go the east road now? . . .
That way a youth went on a morrow
After mirth, and he brought back sorrow
Painted upon his brow
Why go the east road now?

Why go the north road now?
Torn, leaf-strewn, as if scoured by foemen,
Once edging fiefs of my forefolk yeomen,
Fallows fat to the plough:
Why go the north road now?

Why go the west road now?
Thence to us came she, bosom-burning,
Welcome with joyousness returning . . .
—She sleeps under the bough:
Why go the west road now?

Why go the south road now?
That way marched they some are forgetting,
Stark to the moon left, past regretting
Loves who have falsed their vow . . .
Why go the south road now?

Why go any road now?
White stands the handpost for brisk on-bearers,
"Halt!" is the word for wan-cheeked farers
Musing on Whither, and How . . .
Why go any road now?

"Yea: we want new feet now"
Answer the stones. "Want chit-chat, laughter:
Plenty of such to go hereafter
By our tracks, we trow!
We are for new feet now."

During the War

PENANCE

"Why do you sit, O pale thin man,
At the end of the room
By that harpsichord, built on the quaint old plan?
—It is cold as a tomb,
And there's not a spark within the grate;
And the jingling wires
Are as vain desires
That have lagged too late."

"Why do I? Alas, far times ago
A woman lyred here
In the evenfall; one who fain did so
From year to year;
And, in loneliness bending wistfully,
Would wake each note
In sick sad rote,
None to listen or see!

"I would not join. I would not stay,
But drew away,
Though the winter fire beamed brightly . . . Aye!
I do to-day
What I would not then; and the chill old keys,
Like a skull's brown teeth
Loose in their sheath,
Freeze my touch; yes, freeze."

"I LOOK IN HER FACE"

(Song: Minor)

I look in her face and say,
"Sing as you used to sing
About Love's blossoming";
But she hints not Yea or Nay.

"Sing, then, that Love's a pain,
If, Dear, you think it so,
Whether it be or no;"
But dumb her lips remain.

I go to a far-off room,
A faint song ghosts my ear;
Which song I cannot hear,
But it seems to come from a tomb.

AFTER THE WAR

Last Post sounded
Across the mead
To where he loitered

72

With absent heed.
Five years before
In the evening there
Had flown that call
To him and his Dear.
"You'll never come back;
Good-bye!" she had said;
"Here I'll be living,
And my Love dead!"

Those closing minims
Had been as shafts darting
Through him and her pressed
In that last parting;
They thrilled him not now,
In the selfsame place
With the selfsame sun
On his war-seamed face.
"Lurks a god's laughter
In this?" he said,
"That I am the living
And she the dead!"

"IF YOU HAD KNOWN"

If you had known
When listening with her to the far-down moan
Of the white-selvaged and empurpled sea,
And rain came on that did not hinder talk,
Or damp your flashing facile gaiety
In turning home, despite the slow wet walk
By crooked ways, and over stiles of stone;
  If you had known

  You would lay roses,
Fifty years thence, on her monument, that discloses
Its graying shape upon the luxuriant green;
Fifty years thence to an hour, by chance led there,

73

What might have moved you?—yea, had you foreseen
That on the tomb of the selfsame one, gone where
The dawn of every day is as the close is,
   You would lay roses!

1920

THE CHAPEL-ORGANIST

(A.D. 185–)

I've been thinking it through, as I play here to-night, to play never
again,
By the light of that lowering sun peering in at the window-pane,
And over the back-street roofs, throwing shades from the boys of
the chore
In the gallery, right upon me, sitting up to these keys once more . . .

How I used to hear tongues ask, as I sat here when I was new:
"Who is she playing the organ? She touches it mightily true!"
"She travels from Havenpool Town," the deacon would softly speak,
"The stipend can hardly cover her fare hither twice in the week."
 (It fell far short of doing, indeed; but I never told,
For I have craved minstrelsy more than lovers, or beauty, or gold.)

'Twas so he answered at first, but the story grew different later:
"It cannot go on much longer, from what we hear of her now!"
At the meaning wheeze in the words the inquirer would shift his
place
Till he could see round the curtain that screened me from people
below.
"A handsome girl," he would murmur, upstaring, (and so I am).
"But—too much sex in her build; fine eyes, but eyelids too heavy;
A bosom too full for her age; in her lips too voluptuous a look."
(It may be. But who put it there? Assuredly it was not I.)

I went on playing and singing when this I had heard, and more,
Though tears half-blinded me; yes, I remained going on and on,
Just as I used me to chord and to sing at the selfsame time! . . .

74

For it's a contralto—my voice is; they'll hear it again here to-night
In the psalmody notes that I love more than world or than flesh or than life.

Well, the deacon, in fact, that day had learnt new tidings about me;
They troubled his mind not a little, for he was a worthy man.
(He trades as a chemist in High Street, and during the week he had sought
His fellow-deacon, who throve as a book-binder over the way.)
"These are strange rumours," he said. "We must guard the good name of the chapel.
If, sooth, she's of evil report, what else can we do but dismiss her?"
"—But get such another to play here we cannot for double the price!"
It settled the point for the time, and I triumphed awhile in their strait,
And my much-beloved grand semibreves went living on under my fingers.

At length in the congregation more head-shakes and murmurs were rife,
And my dismissal was ruled, though I was not warned of it then.
But a day came when they declared it. The news entered me as a sword;
I was broken; so pallid of face that they thought I should faint, they said.
I rallied. "O, rather than go, I will play you for nothing!" said I.
'Twas in much desperation I spoke it, for bring me to forfeit I could not
Those melodies chorded so richly for which I had laboured and lived.
They paused. And for nothing I played at the chapel through Sundays anon,
Upheld by that art which I loved more than blandishments lavished of men.

But it fell that murmurs again from the flock broke the pastor's peace.
Some member had seen me at Havenpool, comrading close a sea-captain.
(Yes; I was thereto constrained, lacking means for the fare to and fro.)
Yet God knows, if aught He knows ever, I loved the Old-Hundredth, Saint Stephen's,

Mount Zion, New Sabbath, Miles-Lane, Holy Rest, and Arabia, and Eaton,
Above all embraces of body by wooers who sought me and won! ...
Next week 'twas declared I was seen coming home with a lover at dawn.
The deacons insisted then, strong; and forgiveness I did not implore.
I saw all was lost for me, quite, but I made a last bid in my throbs.
High love had been beaten by lust; and the senses had conquered the soul,
But the soul should die game, if I knew it! I turned to my masters and said:
"I yield, Gentlemen, without parlance. But—let me just hymn you once more!
It's a little thing, Sirs, that I ask; and a passion is music with me!"
They saw that consent would cost nothing, and show as good grace, as knew I,
Though tremble I did, and feel sick, as I paused thereat, dumb for their words.
They gloomily nodded assent, saying, "Yes, if you care to. Once more,
And only once more, understand." To that with a bend I agreed.
—"You've a fixed and a far-reaching look," spoke one who had eyed me awhile.
"I've a fixed and a far-reaching plan, and my look only showed it," said I.

This evening of Sunday is come—the last of my functioning here.
 "She plays as if she were possessed!" they exclaim, glancing upward and round.
"Such harmonies I never dreamt the old instrument capable of!"
Meantime the sun lowers and goes; shades deepen; the lights are turned up,
And the people voice out the last singing: tune Tallis: the Evening Hymn.
(I wonder Dissenters sing Ken: it shows them more liberal in spirit
At this little chapel down here than at certain new others I know.)
I sing as I play. Murmurs some one: "No woman's throat richer than hers!"
"True: in these parts, at least," ponder I. "But, my man, you will hear it no more."
And I sing with them onward: "The grave dread as little do I as my bed."

I lift up my feet from the pedals; and then, while my eyes are still wet
From the symphonies born of my fingers, I do that whereon I am set,
And draw from my "full round bosom," (their words; how can I help its heave?)
A bottle blue-coloured and fluted—a vinaigrette, they may conceive—
And before the choir measures my meaning, reads aught in my moves to and fro,
I drink from the phial at a draught, and they think it a pick-me-up; so.
Then I gather my books as to leave, bend over the keys as to pray.
When they come to me motionless, stooping, quick death will have whisked me away.

"Sure, nobody meant her to poison herself in her haste, after all!"
The deacons will say as they carry me down and the night shadows fall,
"Though the charges were true," they will add. "It's a case red as scarlet withal!"
I have never once minced it. Lived chaste I have not. Heaven knows it above! . . .
But past all the heavings of passion—it's music has been my life-love! . . .
That tune did go well—this last playing! . . . I reckon they'll bury me here . . .
Not a soul from the seaport my birthplace—will come, or bestow me . . . a tear.

FETCHING HER

An hour before the dawn,
My friend,
You lit your waiting bedside-lamp,
Your breakfast-fire anon,
And outing into the dark and damp
You saddled, and set on.

Thuswise, before the day,
My friend,
You sought her on her surfy shore,
To fetch her thence away
Unto your own new-builded door
For a staunch lifelong stay.

You said: "It seems to be,
My friend,
That I were bringing to my place
The pure brine breeze, the sea,
The mews—all her old sky and space,
In bringing her with me!"

—But time is prompt to expugn,
My friend,
Such magic-minted conjurings:
The brought breeze fainted soon,
And then the sense of seamews' wings,
And the shore's sibilant tune.

So, it had been more due,
My friend,
Perhaps, had you not pulled this flower
From the craggy nook it knew,
And set it in an alien bower;
But left it where it grew!

"COULD I BUT WILL"

(Song: Verses 1, 3, key major; verse 2, key minor)

Could I but will,
Will to my bent,
I'd have afar ones near me still,
And music of rare ravishment,
In strains that move the toes and heels!
And when the sweethearts sat for rest

The unbetrothed should foot with zest
    Ecstatic reels.

  Could I be head,
    Head-god, "Come, now,
Dear girl," I'd say, "whose flame is fled,
Who liest with linen-banded brow,
Stirred but by shakes from Earth's deep core—"
I'd say to her: "Unshroud and meet
That Love who kissed and called thee Sweet!—
    Yea, come once more!"

  Even half-god power
    In spinning dooms
Had I, this frozen scene should flower,
And sand-swept plains and Arctic glooms
Should green them gay with waving leaves,
Mid which old friends and I would walk
With weightless feet and magic talk
    Uncounted eves.

SHE REVISITS ALONE THE CHURCH
OF HER MARRIAGE

I have come to the church and chancel,
    Where all's the same!
—Brighter and larger in my dreams
Truly it shaped than now, meseems,
    Is its substantial frame.
But, anyhow, I made my vow,
    Whether for praise or blame,
Here in this church and chancel
    Where all's the same.

Where touched the check-floored chancel
    My knees and his?
The step looks shyly at the sun,
And says, "'Twas here the thing was done,

79

For bale or else for bliss!"
Of all those there I least was ware
  Would it be that or this
When touched the check-floored chancel
  My knees and his!

Here in this fateful chancel
  Where all's the same,
I thought the culminant crest of life
Was reached when I went forth the wife
  I was not when I came.
Each commonplace one of my race,
  Some say, has such an aim—
To go from a fateful chancel
  As not the same.

Here, through this hoary chancel
  Where all's the same,
A thrill, a gaiety even, ranged
That morning when it seemed I changed
  My nature with my name.
Though now not fair, though gray my hair,
  He loved me, past proclaim,
Here in this hoary chancel,
  Where all's the same.

AT THE ENTERING OF THE NEW YEAR

I

(OLD STYLE)

Our songs went up and out the chimney,
And roused the home-gone husbandmen;
Our allemands, our heys, poussettings,
Our hands-across and back again,
Sent rhythmic throbbings through the casements

On to the white highway,
Where nighted farers paused and muttered,
  "Keep it up well, do they!"

The contrabasso's measured booming
Sped at each bar to the parish bounds,
To shepherds at their midnight lambings,
To stealthy poachers on their rounds;
And everybody caught full duly
  The notes of our delight,
As Time unrobed the Youth of Promise
  Hailed by our sanguine sight.

II

(NEW STYLE)

We stand in the dusk of a pine-tree limb,
As if to give ear to the muffled peal,
Brought or withheld at the breeze's whim;
But our truest heed is to words that steal
From the mantled ghost that looms in the gray,
And seems, so far as our sense can see,
To feature bereaved Humanity,
As it sighs to the imminent year its say:—

"O stay without, O stay without,
  Calm comely Youth, untasked, untired;
  Though stars irradiate thee about
  Thy entrance here is undesired.
  Open the gate not, mystic one;
Must we avow what we would close confine?
With thee, good friend, we would have converse none,
  Albeit the fault may not be thine."

December 31. During the War

THEY WOULD NOT COME

I travelled to where in her lifetime
She'd knelt at morning prayer,
To call her up as if there;
But she paid no heed to my suing,
As though her old haunt could win not
A thought from her spirit, or care.

I went where my friend had lectioned
The prophets in high declaim,
That my soul's ear the same
Full tones should catch as aforetime;
But silenced by gear of the Present
Was the voice that once there came!

Where the ocean had sprayed our banquet
I stood, to recall it as then:
The same eluding again!
No vision. Shows contingent
Affrighted it further from me
Even than from my home-den.

When I found them no responders,
But fugitives prone to flee
From where they had used to be,
It vouched I had been led hither
As by night wisps in bogland,
And bruised the heart of me!

AFTER A ROMANTIC DAY

The railway bore him through
    An earthen cutting out from a city:
There was no scope for view,
Though the frail light shed by a slim young moon
    Fell like a friendly tune.

82

Fell like a liquid ditty,
And the blank lack of any charm
  Of landscape did no harm.
The bald steep cutting, rigid, rough,
  And moon-lit, was enough
For poetry of place: its weathered face
Formed a convenient sheet whereon
The visions of his mind were drawn.

THE TWO WIVES

(SMOKER'S CLUB-STORY)

I waited at home all the while they were boating together—
  My wife and my near neighbour's wife:
Till there entered a woman I loved more than life,
And we sat and sat on, and beheld the uprising dark weather,
  With a sense that some mischief was rife.

Tidings came that the boat had capsized, and that one of the ladies
  Was drowned—which of them was unknown:
  And I marvelled—my friend's wife?—or was it my own
Who had gone in such wise to the land where the sun as the shade is?
  —We learnt it was his had so gone.

Then I cried in unrest: "He is free! But no good is releasing
  To him as it would be to me!"
  "—But it is," said the woman I loved, quietly.
"How?" I asked her. "—Because he has long loved me too without ceasing,
  And it's just the same thing, don't you see."

"I KNEW A LADY"

(CLUB SONG)

I knew a lady when the days
Grew long, and evenings goldened;
But I was not emboldened
By her prompt eyes and winning ways.

And when old Winter nipt the haws,
"Another's wife I'll be,
And then you'll care for me,"
She said, "and think how sweet I was!"

And soon she shone as another's wife:
As such I often met her,
And sighed, "How I regret her!
My folly cuts me like a knife!"

And then, to-day, her husband came,
And moaned, "Why did you flout her?
Well could I do without her!
For both our burdens you are to blame!"

A HOUSE WITH A HISTORY

There is a house in a city street
Some past ones made their own;
Its floors were criss-crossed by their feet,
And their babblings beat
From ceiling to white hearth-stone.

And who are peopling its parlours now?
Who talk across its floor?
Mere freshlings are they, blank of brow,
Who read not how
Its prime had passed before

Their raw equipments, scenes, and says
Afflicted its memoried face,
That had seen every larger phase
Of human ways
Before these filled the place.

To them that house's tale is theirs,
No former voices call
Aloud therein. Its aspect bears
Their joys and cares
Alone, from wall to wall.

A PROCESSION OF DEAD DAYS

I see the ghost of a perished day;
I know his face, and the feel of his dawn:
'Twas he who took me far away
    To a spot strange and gray:
Look at me, Day, and then pass on,
But come again: yes, come anon!

Enters another into view;
His features are not cold or white,
But rosy as a vein seen through:
    Too soon he smiles adieu.
Adieu, O ghost-day of delight;
But come and grace my dying sight.

Enters the day that brought the kiss:
He brought it in his foggy hand
To where the mumbling river is,
    And the high clematis;
It lent new colour to the land,
And all the boy within me manned.

Ah, this one. Yes, I know his name,
He is the day that wrought a shine
Even on a precinct common and tame,

85

As 'twere of purposed aim.
He shows him as a rainbow sign
Of promise made to me and mine.

The next stands forth in his morning clothes,
And yet, despite their misty blue,
They mark no sombre custom-growths
  That joyous living loathes,
But a meteor act, that left in its queue
A train of sparks my lifetime through.

I almost tremble at his nod—
This next in train—who looks at me
As I were slave, and he were god
  Wielding an iron rod.
I close my eyes; yet still is he
In front there, looking mastery.

In the similitude of a nurse
The phantom of the next one comes:
I did not know what better or worse
  Chancings might bless or curse
When his original glossed the thrums
Of ivy, bringing that which numbs.

Yes; trees were turning in their sleep
Upon their windy pillows of gray
When he stole in. Silent his creep
  On the grassed eastern steep . . .
I shall not soon forget that day,
And what his third hour took away!

HE FOLLOWS HIMSELF

In a heavy time I dogged myself
  Along a louring way,
Till my leading self to my following self
  Said: "Why do you hang on me
    So harassingly?"

"I have watched you, Heart of mine," I cried,
　"So often going astray
And leaving me, that I have pursued,
　Feeling such truancy
　　Ought not to be."

He said no more, and I dogged him on
　From noon to the dun of day
By prowling paths, until anew
　He begged: "Please turn and flee!—
　　What do you see?"

"Methinks I see a man," said I,
　"Dimming his hours to gray.
I will not leave him while I know
　Part of myself is he
　　Who dreams such dree!"

"I go to my old friend's house," he urged,
　"So do not watch me, pray!"
"Well, I will leave you in peace," said I,
　"Though of this poignancy
　　You should fight free:

"Your friend, O other me, is dead;
　You know not what you say."
—"That do I! And at his green-grassed door
　By night's bright galaxy
　　I bend a knee."

—The yew-plumes moved like mockers' beards,
　Though only boughs were they,
And I seemed to go; yet still was there,
　And am, and there haunt we
　　Thus bootlessly.

THE SINGING WOMAN

There was a singing woman
Came riding across the mead
At the time of the mild May weather,
Tameless, tireless;
This song she sung: "I am fair, I am young!"
And many turned to heed.

And the same singing woman
Sat crooning in her need
At the time of the winter weather;
Friendless, fireless,
She sang this song: "Life, thou'rt too long!"
And there was none to heed.

WITHOUT, NOT WITHIN HER

It was what you bore with you, Woman,
    Not inly were,
That throned you from all else human,
    However fair!

It was that strange freshness you carried
    Into a soul
Whereon no thought of yours tarried
    Two moments at all.

And out from his spirit flew death,
    And bale, and ban,
Like the corn-chaff under the breath
    Of the winnowing-fan.

"O I WON'T LEAD A HOMELY LIFE"

(To an old air)

"O I won't lead a homely life
As father's Jack and mother's Jill,
But I will be a fiddler's wife,
With music mine at will!
Just a little tune,
Another one soon,
As I merrily fling my fill!"

And she became a fiddler's Dear,
And merry all day she strove to be;
And he played and played afar and near,
But never at home played he
Any little tune
Or late or soon;
And sunk and sad was she!

IN THE SMALL HOURS

I lay in my bed and fiddled
With a dreamland viol and bow,
And the tunes flew back to my fingers
I had melodied years ago.
It was two or three in the morning
When I fancy-fiddled so
Long reels and country-dances,
And hornpipes swift and slow.

And soon anon came crossing
The chamber in the gray
Figures of jigging fieldfolk—
Saviours of corn and hay—
To the air of "Haste to the Wedding,"
As after a wedding-day;

Yea, up and down the middle
    In windless whirls went they!

There danced the bride and bridegroom,
    And couples in a train,
Gay partners time and travail
    Had longwhiles stilled amain! . . .
It seemed a thing for weeping
    To find, at slumber's wane
And morning's sly increeping,
    That Now, not Then, held reign.

THE LITTLE OLD TABLE

Creak, little wood thing, creak,
When I touch you with elbow or knee;
That is the way you speak
Of one who gave you to me!

You, little table, she brought—
Brought me with her own hand,
As she looked at me with a thought
That I did not understand.

—Whoever owns it anon,
And hears it, will never know
What a history hangs upon
This creak from long ago.

VAGG HOLLOW

Vagg Hollow is a marshy spot on the old Roman Road near Ilchester, where "things" are seen. Merchandise was formerly

fetched inland from the canal-boats at Load-Bridge by waggons this
way.

"What do you see in Vagg Hollow,
Little boy, when you go
In the morning at five on your lonely drive?"
"—I see men's souls, who follow
Till we've passed where the road lies low,
When they vanish at our creaking!

"They are like white faces speaking
Beside and behind the waggon—
One just as father's was when here.
The waggoner drinks from his flagon,
(Or he'd flinch when the Hollow is near)
But he does not give me any.

"Sometimes the faces are many;
But I walk along by the horses,
He asleep on the straw as we jog;
And I hear the loud water-courses,
And the drops from the trees in the fog,
And watch till the day is breaking.

"And the wind out by Tintinhull waking;
I hear in it father's call
As he called when I saw him dying,
And he sat by the fire last Fall,
And mother stood by sighing;
But I'm not afraid at all!"

THE DREAM IS—WHICH?

I am laughing by the brook with her,
  Splashed in its tumbling stir;
And then it is a blankness looms
  As if I walked not there,
Nor she, but found me in haggard rooms,
  And treading a lonely stair.

91

With radiant cheeks and rapid eyes
  We sit where none espies;
Till a harsh change comes edging in
  As no such scene were there,
But winter, and I were bent and thin,
  And cinder-gray my hair.

We dance in heys around the hall,
  Weightless as thistleball;
And then a curtain drops between,
  As if I danced not there,
But wandered through a mounded green
  To find her, I knew where.

March 1913

THE COUNTRY WEDDING

(A FIDDLER'S STORY)

Little fogs were gathered in every hollow,
But the purple hillocks enjoyed fine weather
As we marched with our fiddles over the heather
—How it comes back!—to their wedding that day.

Our getting there brought our neighbours and all, O!
Till, two and two, the couples stood ready.
And her father said: "Souls, for God's sake, be steady!"
And we strung up our fiddles, and sounded out "A."

The groomsman he stared, and said, "You must follow!"
But we'd gone to fiddle in front of the party,
(Our feelings as friends being true and hearty)
And fiddle in front we did—all the way.

Yes, from their door by Mill-tail-Shallow,
And up Styles-Lane, and by Front-Street houses,
Where stood maids, bachelors, and spouses,
Who cheered the songs that we knew how to play.

I bowed the treble before her father,
Michael the tenor in front of the lady,
The bass-viol Reub—and right well played he!—
The serpent Jim; ay, to church and back.

I thought the bridegroom was flurried rather,
As we kept up the tune outside the chancel,
While they were swearing things none can cancel
Inside the walls to our drumstick's whack.

"Too gay!" she pleaded. "Clouds may gather,
And sorrow come." But she gave in, laughing,
And by supper-time when we'd got to the quaffing
Her fears were forgot, and her smiles weren't slack.

A grand wedding 'twas! And what would follow
We never thought. Or that we should have buried her
On the same day with the man that married her,
A day like the first, half hazy, half clear.

Yes: little fogs were in every hollow,
Though the purple hillocks enjoyed fine weather,
When we went to play 'em to church together,
And carried 'em there in an after year.

FIRST OR LAST

(SONG)

If grief come early
Joy comes late,
If joy come early
Grief will wait;
   Aye, my dear and tender!

Wise ones joy them early
While the cheeks are red,
Banish grief till surly
Time has dulled their dread.

And joy being ours
Ere youth has flown,
The later hours
May find us gone;
   Aye, my dear and tender!

LONELY DAYS

Lonely her fate was,
Environed from sight
In the house where the gate was
Past finding at night.
None there to share it,
No one to tell:
Long she'd to bear it,
And bore it well.

Elsewhere just so she
Spent many a day;
Wishing to go she
Continued to stay.
And people without
Basked warm in the air,
But none sought her out,
Or knew she was there.
Even birthdays were passed so,
Sunny and shady:
Years did it last so
For this sad lady.
Never declaring it,
No one to tell,
Still she kept bearing it—
Bore it well.

The days grew chillier,
And then she went
To a city, familiar
In years forespent,

When she walked gaily
Far to and fro,
But now, moving frailly,
Could nowhere go.
The cheerful colour
Of houses she'd known
Had died to a duller
And dingier tone.
Streets were now noisy
Where once had rolled
A few quiet coaches,
Or citizens strolled.
Through the party-wall
Of the memoried spot
They danced at a ball
Who recalled her not.
Tramlines lay crossing
Once gravelled slopes,
Metal rods clanked,
And electric ropes.
So she endured it all,
Thin, thinner wrought,
Until time cured it all,
And she knew nought.
Versified from a Diary.

"WHAT DID IT MEAN?"

What did it mean that noontide, when
You bade me pluck the flower
Within the other woman's bower,
  Whom I knew nought of then?

I thought the flower blushed deeplier—aye,
And as I drew its stalk to me
It seemed to breathe: "I am, I see,
Made use of in a human play."

95

And while I plucked, upstarted sheer
As phantom from the pane thereby
A corpse-like countenance, with eye
That iced me by its baleful peer—
  Silent, as from a bier . . .

When I came back your face had changed,
  It was no face for me;
O did it speak of hearts estranged,
  And deadly rivalry

In times before
  I darked your door,
  To seise me of
  Mere second love,
Which still the haunting first deranged?

AT THE DINNER-TABLE

I sat at dinner in my prime,
And glimpsed my face in the sideboard-glass,
And started as if I had seen a crime,
And prayed the ghastly show might pass.

Wrenched wrinkled features met my sight,
Grinning back to me as my own;
I well-nigh fainted with affright
At finding me a haggard crone.

My husband laughed. He had slily set
A warping mirror there, in whim
To startle me. My eyes grew wet;
I spoke not all the eve to him.

He was sorry, he said, for what he had done,
And took away the distorting glass,
Uncovering the accustomed one;
And so it ended? No, alas,

Fifty years later, when he died,
I sat me in the selfsame chair,
Thinking of him. Till, weary-eyed,
I saw the sideboard facing there;

And from its mirror looked the lean
Thing I'd become, each wrinkle and score
The image of me that I had seen
In jest there fifty years before.

THE MARBLE TABLET

There it stands, though alas, what a little of her
  Shows in its cold white look!
Not her glance, glide, or smile; not a tittle of her
  Voice like the purl of a brook;
    Not her thoughts, that you read like a book.

It may stand for her once in November
  When first she breathed, witless of all;
Or in heavy years she would remember
  When circumstance held her in thrall;
    Or at last, when she answered her call!

Nothing more. The still marble, date-graven,
  Gives all that it can, tersely lined;
That one has at length found the haven
  Which every one other will find;
    With silence on what shone behind.

St. Juliot: September 8, 1916.

THE MASTER AND THE LEAVES

I

We are budding, Master, budding,
We of your favourite tree;
March drought and April flooding
Arouse us merrily,
Our stemlets newly studding;
And yet you do not see!

II

We are fully woven for summer
In stuff of limpest green,
The twitterer and the hummer
Here rest of nights, unseen,
While like a long-roll drummer
The nightjar thrills the treen.

III

We are turning yellow, Master,
And next we are turning red,
And faster then and faster
Shall seek our rooty bed,
All wasted in disaster!
But you lift not your head.

IV

—"I mark your early going,
And that you'll soon be clay,
I have seen your summer showing
As in my youthful day;
But why I seem unknowing
Is too sunk in to say!"

1917

LAST WORDS TO A DUMB FRIEND

Pet was never mourned as you,
Purrer of the spotless hue,
Plumy tail, and wistful gaze
While you humoured our queer ways,
Or outshrilled your morning call
Up the stairs and through the hall—
Foot suspended in its fall—
While, expectant, you would stand
Arched, to meet the stroking hand;
Till your way you chose to wend
Yonder, to your tragic end.

Never another pet for me!
Let your place all vacant be;
Better blankness day by day
Than companion torn away.
Better bid his memory fade,
Better blot each mark he made,
Selfishly escape distress
By contrived forgetfulness,
Than preserve his prints to make
Every morn and eve an ache.

From the chair whereon he sat
Sweep his fur, nor wince thereat;
Rake his little pathways out
Mid the bushes roundabout;
Smooth away his talons' mark
From the claw-worn pine-tree bark,
Where he climbed as dusk embrowned,
Waiting us who loitered round.

Strange it is this speechless thing,
Subject to our mastering,
Subject for his life and food
To our gift, and time, and mood;
Timid pensioner of us Powers,
His existence ruled by ours,
Should—by crossing at a breath
Into safe and shielded death,

By the merely taking hence
Of his insignificance—
Loom as largened to the sense,
Shape as part, above man's will,
Of the Imperturbable.

As a prisoner, flight debarred,
Exercising in a yard,
Still retain I, troubled, shaken,
Mean estate, by him forsaken;
And this home, which scarcely took
Impress from his little look,
By his faring to the Dim
Grows all eloquent of him.

Housemate, I can think you still
Bounding to the window-sill,
Over which I vaguely see
Your small mound beneath the tree,
Showing in the autumn shade
That you moulder where you played.

October 2, 1904

A DRIZZLING EASTER MORNING

And he is risen? Well, be it so . . .
And still the pensive lands complain,
And dead men wait as long ago,
As if, much doubting, they would know
What they are ransomed from, before
They pass again their sheltering door.

I stand amid them in the rain,
While blusters vex the yew and vane;
And on the road the weary wain
Plods forward, laden heavily;
And toilers with their aches are fain
For endless rest—though risen is he.

100

ON ONE WHO LIVED AND DIED WHERE HE WAS BORN

When a night in November
Blew forth its bleared airs
An infant descended
His birth-chamber stairs
For the very first time,
At the still, midnight chime;
All unapprehended
His mission, his aim.—
Thus, first, one November,
An infant descended
The stairs.

On a night in November
Of weariful cares,
A frail aged figure
Ascended those stairs
For the very last time:
All gone his life's prime,
All vanished his vigour,
And fine, forceful frame:
Thus, last, one November
Ascended that figure
Upstairs.

On those nights in November—
Apart eighty years—
The babe and the bent one
Who traversed those stairs
From the early first time
To the last feeble climb—
That fresh and that spent one—
Were even the same:
Yea, who passed in November
As infant, as bent one,
Those stairs.

Wise child of November!
From birth to blanched hairs
Descending, ascending,

Wealth-wantless, those stairs;
Who saw quick in time
As a vain pantomime
Life's tending, its ending,
The worth of its fame.
Wise child of November,
Descending, ascending
Those stairs!

THE SECOND NIGHT

(BALLAD)

I missed one night, but the next I went;
    It was gusty above, and clear;
She was there, with the look of one ill-content,
    And said: "Do not come near!"

—"I am sorry last night to have failed you here,
    And now I have travelled all day;
And it's long rowing back to the West-Hoe Pier,
    So brief must be my stay."

—"O man of mystery, why not say
    Out plain to me all you mean?
Why you missed last night, and must now away
    Is—another has come between!"

—"O woman so mocking in mood and mien,
    So be it!" I replied:
"And if I am due at a differing scene
    Before the dark has died,

"'Tis that, unresting, to wander wide
    Has ever been my plight,
And at least I have met you at Cremyll side
    If not last eve, to-night."

—"You get small rest—that read I quite;
　And so do I, maybe;
Though there's a rest hid safe from sight
　Elsewhere awaiting me!"

A mad star crossed the sky to the sea,
　Wasting in sparks as it streamed,
And when I looked to where stood she
　She had changed, much changed, it seemed:

The sparks of the star in her pupils gleamed,
　She was vague as a vapour now,
And ere of its meaning I had dreamed
　She'd vanished—I knew not how.

I stood on, long; each cliff-top bough,
　Like a cynic nodding there,
Moved up and down, though no man's brow
　But mine met the wayward air.

Still stood I, wholly unaware
　Of what had come to pass,
Or had brought the secret of my new Fair
　To my old Love, alas!

I went down then by crag and grass
　To the boat wherein I had come.
Said the man with the oars: "This news of the lass
　Of Edgcumbe, is sharp for some!

"Yes: found this daybreak, stiff and numb
　On the shore here, whither she'd sped
To meet her lover last night in the glum,
　And he came not, 'tis said.

"And she leapt down, heart-hit. Pity she's dead:
　So much for the faithful-bent!" . . .
I looked, and again a star overhead
　Shot through the firmament.

SHE WHO SAW NOT

"Did you see something within the house
That made me call you before the red sunsetting?
Something that all this common scene endows
With a richened impress there can be no forgetting?"

"—I have found nothing to see therein,
O Sage, that should have made you urge me to enter,
Nothing to fire the soul, or the sense to win:
I rate you as a rare misrepresenter!"

"—Go anew, Lady,—in by the right . . .
Well: why does your face not shine like the face of Moses?"
"—I found no moving thing there save the light
And shadow flung on the wall by the outside roses."

"—Go yet once more, pray. Look on a seat."
"—I go . . . O Sage, it's only a man that sits there
With eyes on the sun. Mute,—average head to feet."
"—No more?"—"No more. Just one the place befits there,

"As the rays reach in through the open door,
And he looks at his hand, and the sun glows through his
fingers,
While he's thinking thoughts whose tenour is no more
To me than the swaying rose-tree shade that lingers."

No more. And years drew on and on
Till no sun came, dank fogs the house enfolding;
And she saw inside, when the form in the flesh had gone,
As a vision what she had missed when the real beholding.

THE OLD WORKMAN

"Why are you so bent down before your time,
Old mason? Many have not left their prime

So far behind at your age, and can still
   Stand full upright at will."

He pointed to the mansion-front hard by,
And to the stones of the quoin against the sky;
"Those upper blocks," he said, "that there you see,
   It was that ruined me."

There stood in the air up to the parapet
Crowning the corner height, the stones as set
By him—ashlar whereon the gales might drum
   For centuries to come.

"I carried them up," he said, "by a ladder there;
The last was as big a load as I could bear;
But on I heaved; and something in my back
   Moved, as 'twere with a crack.

"So I got crookt. I never lost that sprain;
And those who live there, walled from wind and rain
By freestone that I lifted, do not know
   That my life's ache came so.

"They don't know me, or even know my name,
But good I think it, somehow, all the same
To have kept 'em safe from harm, and right and tight,
   Though it has broke me quite.

"Yes; that I fixed it firm up there I am proud,
Facing the hail and snow and sun and cloud,
And to stand storms for ages, beating round
   When I lie underground."

THE SAILOR'S MOTHER

"O whence do you come,
Figure in the night-fog that chills me numb?"

105

"I come to you across from my house up there,
And I don't mind the brine-mist clinging to me
    That blows from the quay,
For I heard him in my chamber, and thought you unaware."

 "But what did you hear,
That brought you blindly knocking in this middle-watch so
drear?"

"My sailor son's voice as 'twere calling at your door,
And I don't mind my bare feet clammy on the stones,
    And the blight to my bones,
For he only knows of this house I lived in before."

 "Nobody's nigh,
Woman like a skeleton, with socket-sunk eye."

"Ah—nobody's nigh! And my life is drearisome,
And this is the old home we loved in many a day
    Before he went away;
And the salt fog mops me. And nobody's come!"

From "To Please his Wife."

OUTSIDE THE CASEMENT

(A REMINISCENCE OF THE WAR)

    We sat in the room
    And praised her whom
We saw in the portico-shade outside:
    She could not hear
    What was said of her,
But smiled, for its purport we did not hide.

    Then in was brought
    That message, fraught
With evil fortune for her out there,

Whom we loved that day
More than any could say,
And would fain have fenced from a waft of care.

And the question pressed
Like lead on each breast,
Should we cloak the tidings, or call her and tell?
It was too intense
A choice for our sense,
As we pondered and watched her we loved so well.

Yea, spirit failed us
At what assailed us;
How long, while seeing what soon must come,
Should we counterfeit
No knowledge of it,
And stay the stroke that would blanch and numb?

And thus, before
For evermore
Joy left her, we practised to beguile
Her innocence when
She now and again
Looked in, and smiled us another smile.

THE PASSER-BY

(L. H. RECALLS HER ROMANCE)

He used to pass, well-trimmed and brushed,
  My window every day,
And when I smiled on him he blushed,
That youth, quite as a girl might; aye,
  In the shyest way.

Thus often did he pass hereby,
  That youth of bounding gait,
Until the one who blushed was I,

And he became, as here I sate,
  My joy, my fate.

And now he passes by no more,
  That youth I loved too true!
I grieve should he, as here of yore,
Pass elsewhere, seated in his view,
  Some maiden new!

If such should be, alas for her!
  He'll make her feel him dear,
Become her daily comforter,
Then tire him of her beauteous gear,
  And disappear!

"I WAS THE MIDMOST"

I was the midmost of my world
  When first I frisked me free,
For though within its circuit gleamed
  But a small company,
And I was immature, they seemed
  To bend their looks on me.

She was the midmost of my world
  When I went further forth,
And hence it was that, whether I turned
  To south, east, west, or north,
Beams of an all-day Polestar burned
  From that new axe of earth.

Where now is midmost in my world?
  I trace it not at all:
No midmost shows it here, or there,
  When wistful voices call
"We are fain! We are fain!" from everywhere
  On Earth's bewildering ball!

A SOUND IN THE NIGHT

(WOODSFORD CASTLE: 17–)

"What do I catch upon the night-wind, husband?—
What is it sounds in this house so eerily?
It seems to be a woman's voice: each little while I hear it,
    And it much troubles me!"

"'Tis but the eaves dripping down upon the plinth-slopes:
Letting fancies worry thee!—sure 'tis a foolish thing,
When we were on'y coupled half-an-hour before the
noontide,
    And now it's but evening."

"Yet seems it still a woman's voice outside the castle,
husband,
And 'tis cold to-night, and rain beats, and this is a lonely
place.
Didst thou fathom much of womankind in travel or
adventure
    Ere ever thou sawest my face?"

"It may be a tree, bride, that rubs his arms acrosswise,
If it is not the eaves-drip upon the lower slopes,
Or the river at the bend, where it whirls about the hatches
    Like a creature that sighs and mopes."

"Yet it still seems to me like the crying of a woman,
And it saddens me much that so piteous a sound
On this my bridal night when I would get agone from sorrow
    Should so ghost-like wander round!"

"To satisfy thee, Love, I will strike the flint-and-steel, then,
And set the rush-candle up, and undo the door,
And take the new horn-lantern that we bought upon our
journey,
    And throw the light over the moor."

He struck a light, and breeched and booted in the further
chamber,
And lit the new horn-lantern and went from her sight,

109

And vanished down the turret; and she heard him pass the postern,
   And go out into the night.

She listened as she lay, till she heard his step returning,
And his voice as he unclothed him: "'Twas nothing, as I said,
But the nor'-west wind a-blowing from the moor ath'art the river,
   And the tree that taps the gurgoyle-head."

"Nay, husband, you perplex me; for if the noise I heard here,
Awaking me from sleep so, were but as you avow,
The rain-fall, and the wind, and the tree-bough, and the river,
   Why is it silent now?

"And why is thy hand and thy clasping arm so shaking,
And thy sleeve and tags of hair so muddy and so wet,
And why feel I thy heart a-thumping every time thou kissest me,
   And thy breath as if hard to get?"

He lay there in silence for a while, still quickly breathing,
Then started up and walked about the room resentfully:
"O woman, witch, whom I, in sooth, against my will have wedded,
   Why castedst thou thy spells on me?

"There was one I loved once: the cry you heard was her cry:
She came to me to-night, and her plight was passing sore,
As no woman . . . Yea, and it was e'en the cry you heard, wife,
   But she will cry no more!

"And now I can't abide thee: this place, it hath a curse on't,
This farmstead once a castle: I'll get me straight away!"
He dressed this time in darkness, unspeaking, as she listened,
   And went ere the dawn turned day.

They found a woman's body at a spot called Rocky Shallow,
Where the Froom stream curves amid the moorland, washed aground,

And they searched about for him, the yeoman, who had
darkly known her,
    But he could not be found.

And the bride left for good-and-all the farmstead once a
castle,
And in a county far away lives, mourns, and sleeps alone,
And thinks in windy weather that she hears a woman crying,
    And sometimes an infant's moan.

ON A DISCOVERED CURL OF HAIR

When your soft welcomings were said,
This curl was waving on your head,
And when we walked where breakers dinned
It sported in the sun and wind,
And when I had won your words of grace
It brushed and clung about my face.
Then, to abate the misery
Of absentness, you gave it me.

Where are its fellows now? Ah, they
For brightest brown have donned a gray,
And gone into a caverned ark,
Ever unopened, always dark!

Yet this one curl, untouched of time,
Beams with live brown as in its prime,
So that it seems I even could now
Restore it to the living brow
By bearing down the western road
Till I had reached your old abode.

February 1913

AN OLD LIKENESS

(RECALLING R. T.)

Who would have thought
That, not having missed her
Talks, tears, laughter
In absence, or sought
To recall for so long
Her gamut of song;
Or ever to waft her
Signal of aught
That she, fancy-fanned,
Would well understand,
I should have kissed her
Picture when scanned
Yawning years after!

Yet, seeing her poor
Dim-outlined form
Chancewise at night-time,
Some old allure
Came on me, warm,
Fresh, pleadful, pure,
As in that bright time
At a far season
Of love and unreason,
And took me by storm
Here in this blight-time!
And thus it arose
That, yawning years after
Our early flows
Of wit and laughter,
And framing of rhymes
At idle times,
At sight of her painting,
Though she lies cold
In churchyard mould,
I took its feinting
As real, and kissed it,
As if I had wist it
Herself of old.

HER APOTHEOSIS

"Secretum meum mihi"

(FADED WOMAN'S SONG)

There was a spell of leisure,
No record vouches when;
With honours, praises, pleasure
To womankind from men.

But no such lures bewitched me,
No hand was stretched to raise,
No gracious gifts enriched me,
No voices sang my praise.

Yet an iris at that season
Amid the accustomed slight
From denseness, dull unreason,
Ringed me with living light.

"SACRED TO THE MEMORY"

(MARY H.)

That "Sacred to the Memory"
Is clearly carven there I own,
And all may think that on the stone
The words have been inscribed by me
In bare conventionality.

They know not and will never know
That my full script is not confined
To that stone space, but stands deep lined
Upon the landscape high and low
Wherein she made such worthy show.

113

TO A WELL-NAMED DWELLING

Glad old house of lichened stonework,
What I owed you in my lone work,
  Noon and night!
Whensoever faint or ailing,
Letting go my grasp and failing,
  You lent light.

How by that fair title came you?
Did some forward eye so name you
  Knowing that one,
Sauntering down his century blindly,
Would remark your sound, so kindly,
  And be won?

Smile in sunlight, sleep in moonlight,
Bask in April, May, and June-light,
  Zephyr-fanned;
Let your chambers show no sorrow,
Blanching day, or stuporing morrow,
  While they stand.

THE WHIPPER-IN

My father was the whipper-in,—
  Is still—if I'm not misled?
And now I see, where the hedge is thin,
  A little spot of red;
  Surely it is my father
  Going to the kennel-shed!

"I cursed and fought my father—aye,
  And sailed to a foreign land;
And feeling sorry, I'm back, to stay,
  Please God, as his helping hand.
  Surely it is my father
  Near where the kennels stand?"

114

"—True. Whipper-in he used to be
    For twenty years or more;
And you did go away to sea
    As youths have done before.
    Yes, oddly enough that red there
    Is the very coat he wore.

"But he—he's dead; was thrown somehow,
    And gave his back a crick,
And though that is his coat, 'tis now
    The scarecrow of a rick;
    You'll see when you get nearer—
    'Tis spread out on a stick.

"You see, when all had settled down
    Your mother's things were sold,
And she went back to her own town,
    And the coat, ate out with mould,
    Is now used by the farmer
    For scaring, as 'tis old."

A MILITARY APPOINTMENT

(SCHERZANDO)

"So back you have come from the town, Nan, dear!
And have you seen him there, or near—
    That soldier of mine—
Who long since promised to meet me here?"

"—O yes, Nell: from the town I come,
And have seen your lover on sick-leave home—
    That soldier of yours—
Who swore to meet you, or Strike-him-dumb;

"But has kept himself of late away;
Yet,—in short, he's coming, I heard him say—
    That lover of yours—
To this very spot on this very day."

115

"—Then I'll wait, I'll wait, through wet or dry!
I'll give him a goblet brimming high—
    This lover of mine—
And not of complaint one word or sigh!"

"—Nell, him I have chanced so much to see,
That—he has grown the lover of me!—
    That lover of yours—
And it's here our meeting is planned to be."

THE MILESTONE BY THE RABBIT-BURROW

(ON YELL'HAM HILL)

In my loamy nook
As I dig my hole
I observe men look
At a stone, and sigh
As they pass it by
To some far goal.

Something it says
To their glancing eyes
That must distress
The frail and lame,
And the strong of frame
Gladden or surprise.

Do signs on its face
Declare how far
Feet have to trace
Before they gain
Some blest champaign
Where no gins are?

THE LAMENT OF THE LOOKING-GLASS

Words from the mirror softly pass
To the curtains with a sigh:
"Why should I trouble again to glass
These smileless things hard by,
Since she I pleasured once, alas,
Is now no longer nigh!"

"I've imaged shadows of coursing cloud,
And of the plying limb
On the pensive pine when the air is loud
With its aerial hymn;
But never do they make me proud
To catch them within my rim!

"I flash back phantoms of the night
That sometimes flit by me,
I echo roses red and white—
The loveliest blooms that be—
But now I never hold to sight
So sweet a flower as she."

CROSS-CURRENTS

They parted—a pallid, trembling I pair,
And rushing down the lane
He left her lonely near me there;
—I asked her of their pain.

"It is for ever," at length she said,
"His friends have schemed it so,
That the long-purposed day to wed
Never shall we two know."

"In such a cruel case," said I,
"Love will contrive a course?"

"—Well, no . . . A thing may underlie,
    Which robs that of its force;

"A thing I could not tell him of,
    Though all the year I have tried;
This: never could I have given him love,
    Even had I been his bride.

"So, when his kinsfolk stop the way
    Point-blank, there could not be
A happening in the world to-day
    More opportune for me!

"Yet hear—no doubt to your surprise—
    I am sorry, for his sake,
That I have escaped the sacrifice
    I was prepared to make!"

THE OLD NEIGHBOUR AND THE NEW

'Twas to greet the new rector I called I here,
    But in the arm-chair I see
My old friend, for long years installed here,
    Who palely nods to me.

The new man explains what he's planning
    In a smart and cheerful tone,
And I listen, the while that I'm scanning
    The figure behind his own.

The newcomer urges things on me;
    I return a vague smile thereto,
The olden face gazing upon me
    Just as it used to do!

And on leaving I scarcely remember
    Which neighbour to-day I have seen,
The one carried out in September,
    Or him who but entered yestreen.

THE CHOSEN

"Ατινά ἐστιν ἀλληγορούμενα

"A woman for whom great gods might strive!"
  I said, and kissed her there:
And then I thought of the other five,
  And of how charms outwear.

I thought of the first with her eating eyes,
And I thought of the second with hers, green-gray,
And I thought of the third, experienced, wise,
And I thought of the fourth who sang all day.

And I thought of the fifth, whom I'd called a jade,
  And I thought of them all, tear-fraught;
And that each had shown her a passable maid,
  Yet not of the favour sought.

So I traced these words on the bark of a beech,
Just at the falling of the mast:
"After scanning five; yes, each and each,
I've found the woman desired—at last!"

"—I feel a strange benumbing spell,
  As one ill-wished!" said she.
And soon it seemed that something fell
  Was starving her love for me.

"I feel some curse. O, five were there?"
And wanly she swerved, and went away.
I followed sick: night numbed the air,
And dark the mournful moorland lay.

I cried: "O darling, turn your head!"
  But never her face I viewed;
"O turn, O turn!" again I said,
  And miserably pursued.

At length I came to a Christ-cross stone
Which she had passed without discern;
And I knelt upon the leaves there strown,
And prayed aloud that she might turn.

119

I rose, and looked; and turn she did;
  I cried, "My heart revives!"
"Look more," she said. I looked as bid;
  Her face was all the five's.

All the five women, clear come back,
I saw in her—with her made one,
The while she drooped upon the track,
And her frail term seemed well-nigh run.

She'd half forgot me in her change;
  "Who are you? Won't you say
Who you may be, you man so strange,
  Following since yesterday?"

I took the composite form she was,
And carried her to an arbour small,
Not passion-moved, but even because
In one I could atone to all.

And there she lies, and there I tend,
  Till my life's threads unwind,
A various womanhood in blend—
  Not one, but all combined.

THE INSCRIPTION

(A TALE)

Sir John was entombed, and the crypt was closed, and she,
Like a soul that could meet no more the sight of the sun,
Inclined her in weepings and prayings continually,
  As his widowed one.

And to pleasure her in her sorrow, and fix his name
As a memory Time's fierce frost should never kill,
She caused to be richly chased a brass to his fame,
  Which should link them still;

120

For she bonded her name with his own on the brazen page,
As if dead and interred there with him, and cold, and numb,
  (Omitting the day of her dying and year of her age
    Till her end should come;)

And implored good people to pray "Of their Charytie
For these twaine Soules,"—yea, she who did last remain
Forgoing Heaven's bliss if ever with spouse should she
    Again have lain.

Even there, as it first was set, you may see it now,
Writ in quaint Church text, with the date of her death left
bare,
In the aged Estminster aisle, where the folk yet bow
    Themselves in prayer.

Thereafter some years slid, till there came a day
When it slowly began to be marked of the standers-by
That she would regard the brass, and would bend away
    With a drooping sigh.

Now the lady was fair as any the eye might scan
Through a summer day of roving—a type at whose lip
Despite her maturing seasons, no meet man
    Would be loth to sip.

And her heart was stirred with a lightning love to its pith
For a newcomer who, while less in years, was one
Full eager and able to make her his own forthwith,
    Restrained of none.

But she answered Nay, death-white; and still as he urged
She adversely spake, overmuch as she loved the while,
Till he pressed for why, and she led with the face of one
scourged
    To the neighbouring aisle,

And showed him the words, ever gleaming upon her pew,
Memorizing her there as the knight's eternal wife,
Or falsing such, debarred inheritance due
    Of celestial life.

He blenched, and reproached her that one yet undeceased
Should bury her future—that future which none can spell;

And she wept, and purposed anon to inquire of the priest
    If the price were hell

Of her wedding in face of the record. Her lover agreed,
And they parted before the brass with a shudderful kiss,
For it seemed to flash out on their impulse of passionate need,
    "Mock ye not this!"

Well, the priest, whom more perceptions moved than one,
Said she erred at the first to have written as if she were dead
Her name and adjuration; but since it was done
    Nought could be said

Save that she must abide by the pledge, for the peace of her soul,
And so, by her life, maintain the apostrophe good,
If she wished anon to reach the coveted goal
    Of beatitude.

To erase from the consecrate text her prayer as there prayed
Would aver that, since earth's joys most drew her, past doubt,
Friends' prayers for her joy above by Jesu's aid
    Could be done without.

Moreover she thought of the laughter, the shrug, the jibe
That would rise at her back in the nave when she should pass
As another's avowed by the words she had chosen to inscribe
    On the changeless brass.

And so for months she replied to her Love: "No, no";
While sorrow was gnawing her beauties ever and more,
Till he, long-suffering and weary, grew to show
    Less warmth than before.

And, after an absence, wrote words absolute:
That he gave her till Midsummer morn to make her mind clear;
And that if, by then, she had not said Yea to his suit,
    He should wed elsewhere.

Thence on, at unwonted times through the lengthening days

She was seen in the church—at dawn, or when the sun dipt
And the moon rose, standing with hands joined, blank of
gaze,
  Before the script.

She thinned as he came not; shrank like a creature that
cowers
As summer drew nearer; but still had not promised to wed,
When, just at the zenith of June, in the still night hours,
  She was missed from her bed.

"The church!" they whispered with qualms; "where often she
sits."
They found her: facing the brass there, else seeing none,
But feeling the words with her finger, gibbering in fits;
  And she knew them not one.

And so she remained, in her handmaids' charge; late, soon,
Tracing words in the air with her finger, as seen that night—
Those incised on the brass—till at length unwatched one
noon,
  She vanished from sight.

And, as talebearers tell, thence on to her last-taken breath
Was unseen, save as wraith that in front of the brass made
moan;
So that ever the way of her life and the time of her death
  Remained unknown.

And hence, as indited above, you may read even now
The quaint church-text, with the date of her death left bare,
In the aged Estminster aisle, where folk yet bow
  Themselves in prayer.

October 30, 1907

THE MARBLE-STREETED TOWN

I reach the marble-streeted town,
  Whose "Sound" outbreathes its air
    Of sharp sea-salts;
I see the movement up and down
  As when she was there.
Ships of all countries come and go,
  The bandsmen boom in the sun
    A throbbing waltz;
The schoolgirls laugh along the Hoe
  As when she was one.

I move away as the music rolls:
  The place seems not to mind
    That she—of old
The brightest of its native souls—
  Left it behind!
Over this green aforedays she
  On light treads went and came,
    Yea, times untold;
Yet none here knows her history—
  Has heard her name.

Plymouth (1914?)

A WOMAN DRIVING

How she held up the horses' heads,
  Firm-lipped, with steady rein,
Down that grim steep the coastguard treads,
  Till all was safe again!

With form erect and keen contour
  She passed against the sea,
And, dipping into the chine's obscure,
  Was seen no more by me.

124

To others she appeared anew
At times of dusky light,
But always, so they told, withdrew
From close and curious sight.

Some said her silent wheels would roll
Rutless on softest loam,
And even that her steeds' footfall
Sank not upon the foam.

Where drives she now? It may be where
No mortal horses are,
But in a chariot of the air
Towards some radiant star.

A WOMAN'S TRUST

If he should live a thousand years
He'd find it not again
That scorn of him by men
Could less disturb a woman's trust
In him as a steadfast star which must
Rise scathless from the nether spheres:
If he should live a thousand years
He'd find it not again.

She waited like a little child,
Unchilled by damps of doubt,
While from her eyes looked out
A confidence sublime as Spring's
When stressed by Winter's loiterings.
Thus, howsoever the wicked wiled,
She waited like a little child
Unchilled by damps of doubt.

Through cruel years and crueller
Thus she believed in him

125

And his aurore, so dim;
That, after fenweeds, flowers would blow;
And above all things did she show
Her faith in his good faith with her;
Through cruel years and crueller
Thus she believed in him!

BEST TIMES

We went a day's excursion to the stream,
Basked by the bank, and bent to the ripple-gleam,
And I did not know
That life would show,
However it might flower, no finer glow.

I walked in the Sunday sunshine by the road
That wound towards the wicket of your abode,
And I did not think
That life would shrink
To nothing ere it shed a rosier pink.

Unlooked for I arrived on a rainy night,
And you hailed me at the door by the swaying light,
And I full forgot
That life might not
Again be touching that ecstatic height.

And that calm eve when you walked up the stair,
After a gaiety prolonged and rare,
No thought soever
That you might never
Walk down again, struck me as I stood there.
Rewritten from an old draft.

THE CASUAL ACQUAINTANCE

While he was here in breath and bone,
  To speak to and to see,
Would I had known—more clearly known—
  What that man did for me

When the wind scraped a minor lay,
  And the spent west from white
To gray turned tiredly, and from gray
  To broadest bands of night!

But I saw not, and he saw not
  What shining life-tides flowed
To me-ward from his casual jot
  Of service on that road.

He would have said: "'Twas nothing new;
  We all do what we can;
'Twas only what one man would do
  For any other man."

Now that I gauge his goodliness
  He's slipped from human eyes;
And when he passed there's none can guess,
  Or point out where he lies.

INTRA SEPULCHRUM

What curious things we said,
  What curious things we did
Up there in the world we walked till dead
  Our kith and kin amid!

How we played at love,
  And its wildness, weakness, woe;

127

Yes, played thereat far more than enough
  As it turned out, I trow!

Played at believing in gods
  And observing the ordinances,
I for your sake in impossible codes
  Right ready to acquiesce.

Thinking our lives unique,
  Quite quainter than usual kinds,
We held that we could not abide a week
  The tether of typic minds.

—Yet people who day by day
  Pass by and look at us
From over the wall in a casual way
  Are of this unconscious.

And feel, if anything,
  That none can be buried here
Removed from commonest fashioning,
  Or lending note to a bier:

No twain who in heart-heaves proved
  Themselves at all adept,
Who more than many laughed and loved,
  Who more than many wept,

Or were as sprites or elves
  Into blind matter hurled,
Or ever could have been to themselves
  The centre of the world.

THE WHITEWASHED WALL

Why does she turn in that shy soft way
  Whenever she stirs the fire,
And kiss to the chimney-corner wall,

As if entranced to admire
Its whitewashed bareness more than the sight
   Of a rose in richest green?
I have known her long, but this raptured rite
   I never before have seen.

—Well, once when her son cast his shadow there,
   A friend took a pencil and drew him
Upon that flame-lit wall. And the lines
   Had a lifelike semblance to him.
And there long stayed his familiar look;
   But one day, ere she knew,
The whitener came to cleanse the nook,
   And covered the face from view.

"Yes," he said: "My brush goes on with a rush,
   And the draught is buried under;
When you have to whiten old cots and brighten,
   What else can you do, I wonder?"
But she knows he's there. And when she yearns
   For him, deep in the labouring night,
She sees him as close at hand, and turns
   To him under his sheet of white.

JUST THE SAME

I sat. It all was past;
Hope never would hail again;
Fair days had ceased at a blast,
The world was a darkened den.

The beauty and dream were gone,
And the halo in which I had hied
So gaily gallantly on
Had suffered blot and died!

I went forth, heedless whither,
In a cloud too black for name:

—People frisked hither and thither;
The world was just the same.

THE LAST TIME

The kiss had been given and taken,
And gathered to many past:
It never could reawaken;
But you heard none say: "It's the last!"

The clock showed the hour and the minute,
But you did not turn and look:
You read no finis in it,
As at closing of a book.

But you read it all too rightly
When, at a time anon,
A figure lay stretched out whitely,
And you stood looking thereon.

THE SEVEN TIMES

The dark was thick. A boy he seemed at that time
  Who trotted by me with uncertain air;
"I'll tell my tale," he murmured, "for I fancy
  A friend goes there? ... "

Then thus he told. "I reached—'twas for the first time—
  A dwelling. Life was clogged in me with care;
I thought not I should meet an eyesome maiden,
  But found one there.

"I entered on the precincts for the second time—
  'Twas an adventure fit and fresh and fair—

I slackened in my footsteps at the porchway,
  And found her there.

"I rose and travelled thither for the third time,
  The hope-hues growing gayer and yet gayer
As I hastened round the boscage of the outskirts,
  And found her there.

"I journeyed to the place again the fourth time
  (The best and rarest visit of the rare,
As it seemed to me, engrossed about these goings),
  And found her there.

"When I bent me to my pilgrimage the fifth time
  (Soft-thinking as I journeyed I would dare
A certain word at token of good auspice),
  I found her there.

"That landscape did I traverse for the sixth time,
  And dreamed on what we purposed to prepare;
I reached a tryst before my journey's end came,
  And found her there.

"I went again—long after—aye, the seventh time;
  The look of things was sinister and bare
As I caught no customed signal, heard no voice call,
  Nor found her there.

"And now I gad the globe—day, night, and any time,
  To light upon her hiding unaware,
And, maybe, I shall nigh me to some nymph-niche,
  And find her there!"

"But how," said I, "has your so little lifetime
  Given roomage for such loving, loss, despair?
A boy so young!" Forthwith I turned my lantern
  Upon him there.

His head was white. His small form, fine aforetime,
  Was shrunken with old age and battering wear,
An eighty-years long plodder saw I pacing
  Beside me there.

THE SUN'S LAST LOOK ON THE COUNTRY GIRL

(M. H.)

The sun threw down a radiant spot
  On the face in the winding-sheet—
The face it had lit when a babe's in its cot;
And the sun knew not, and the face knew not
  That soon they would no more meet.

Now that the grave has shut its door,
  And lets not in one ray,
Do they wonder that they meet no more—
That face and its beaming visitor—
  That met so many a day?

December 1915

IN A LONDON FLAT

I

"You look like a widower," she said
Through the folding-doors with a laugh from the bed,
As he sat by the fire in the outer room,
Reading late on a night of gloom,
And a cab-hack's wheeze, and the clap of its feet
In its breathless pace on the smooth wet street,
Were all that came to them now and then . . .
"You really do!" she quizzed again.

II

And the Spirits behind the curtains heard,
And also laughed, amused at her word,
And at her light-hearted view of him.

132

·"Let's get him made so—just for a whim!"
Said the Phantom Ironic. "'Twould serve her right
If we coaxed the Will to do it some night."
"O pray not!" pleaded the younger one,
The Sprite of the Pities. "She said it in fun!"

III

But so it befell, whatever the cause,
That what she had called him he next year was;
And on such a night, when she lay elsewhere,
He, watched by those Phantoms, again sat there,
And gazed, as if gazing on far faint shores,
At the empty bed through the folding-doors
As he remembered her words; and wept
That she had forgotten them where she slept.

DRAWING DETAILS IN AN OLD CHURCH

I hear the bell-rope sawing,
And the oil-less axle grind,
As I sit alone here drawing
What some Gothic brain designed;
And I catch the toll that follows
    From the lagging bell,
Ere it spreads to hills and hollows
Where the parish people dwell.

I ask not whom it tolls for,
Incurious who he be;
So, some morrow, when those knolls for
One unguessed, sound out for me,
A stranger, loitering under
    In nave or choir,
May think, too, "Whose, I wonder?"
But care not to inquire.

RAKE-HELL MUSES

Yes; since she knows not need,
　　Nor walks in blindness,
　Were her poor footsteps seeking
　　A true thing tell:

Which would be truth, indeed,
　　Though worse in speaking,
　Were her poor footsteps seeking
　　A pauper's cell.

I judge, then, better far
　　She now have sorrow,
　Than gladness that to-morrow
　　Might know its knell.—

It may be men there are
　　Could make of union
　A lifelong sweet communion—
　　A passioned spell;

But I, to save her name
　　And bring salvation
　By altar-affirmation
　　And bridal bell;

I, by whose rash unshame
　　These tears come to her:—
　My faith would more undo her
　　Than my farewell!

Chained to me, year by year
　　My moody madness
　Would wither her old gladness
　　Like famine fell.

She'll take the ill that's near,
　　And bear the blaming.
　'Twill pass. Full soon her shaming
　　They'll cease to yell.

Our unborn, first her moan,
Will grow her guerdon,
Until from blot and burden
A joyance swell;

In that therein she'll own
My good part wholly,
My evil staining solely
My own vile vell.

Of the disgrace, may be
"He shunned to share it,
Being false," they'll say. I'll bear it;
Time will dispel

The calumny, and prove
This much about me,
That she lives best without me
Who would live well.

That, this once, not self-love
But good intention
Pleads that against convention
We two rebel.

For, is one moonlight dance,
One midnight passion,
A rock whereon to fashion
Life's citadel?

Prove they their power to prance
Life's miles together
From upper slope to nether
Who trip an ell?

—Years hence, or now apace,
May tongues be calling
News of my further falling
Sinward pell-mell:

Then this great good will grace
Our lives' division,

She's saved from more misprision
Though I plumb hell.

189–

THE COLOUR

(The following lines are partly made up, partly remembered from a Wessex folk-rhyme)

"What shall I bring you?
Please will white do
Best for your wearing
The long day through?"
"—White is for weddings,
Weddings, weddings,
White is for weddings,
And that won't do."

"What shall I bring you?
Please will red do
Best for your wearing
The long day through?"
" —Red is for soldiers,
Soldiers, soldiers,
Red is for soldiers,
And that won't do."

"What shall I bring you?
Please will blue do
Best for your wearing
The long day through?"
"—Blue is for sailors,
Sailors, sailors,
Blue is for sailors,
And that won't do.

"What shall I bring you?

Please will green do
Best for your wearing
The long day through?"
"—Green is for mayings,
Mayings, mayings,
Green is for mayings,
And that won't do."

"What shall I bring you
Then? Will black do
Best for your wearing
The long day through?"
"—Black is for mourning,
Mourning, mourning,
Black is for mourning,
And black will do."

MURMURS IN THE GLOOM

(NOCTURNE)

I wayfared at the nadir of the sun
Where populations meet, though seen of none;
And millions seemed to sigh around
As though their haunts were nigh around,
And unknown throngs to cry around
Of things late done.

"O Seers, who well might high ensample show"
(Came throbbing past in plainsong small and slow),
"Leaders who lead us aimlessly,
Teachers who train us shamelessly,
Why let ye smoulder flamelessly
The truths ye trow?

"Ye scribes, that urge the old medicament,
Whose fusty vials have long dried impotent,
Why prop ye meretricious things,

Denounce the sane as vicious things,
And call outworn factitious things
                    Expedient?

"O Dynasties that sway and shake us so,
Why rank your magnanimities so low
That grace can smooth no waters yet,
But breathing threats and slaughters yet
Ye grieve Earth's sons and daughters yet
                    As long ago?

"Live there no heedful ones of searching sight,
Whose accents might be oracles that smite
To hinder those who frowardly
Conduct us, and untowardly;
To lead the nations vawardly
                    From gloom to light?"

September 22, 1899

EPITAPH

I never cared for Life: Life cared for me,
And hence I owed it some fidelity.
It now says, "Cease; at length thou hast learnt to grind
Sufficient toll for an unwilling mind,
And I dismiss thee—not without regard
That thou didst ask no ill-advised reward,
Nor sought in me much more than thou couldst find."

AN ANCIENT TO ANCIENTS

Where once we danced, where once we sang,
    Gentlemen,
The floors are sunken, cobwebs hang,
And cracks creep; worms have fed upon
The doors. Yea, sprightlier times were then
Than now, with harps and tabrets gone,
    Gentlemen!

Where once we rowed, where once we sailed,
    Gentlemen,
And damsels took the tiller, veiled
Against too strong a stare (God wot
Their fancy, then or anywhen!)
Upon that shore we are clean forgot,
    Gentlemen!

We have lost somewhat, afar and near,
    Gentlemen,
The thinning of our ranks each year
Affords a hint we are nigh undone,
That we shall not be ever again
The marked of many, loved of one,
    Gentlemen.

In dance the polka hit our wish,
    Gentlemen,
The paced quadrille, the spry schottische,
"Sir Roger."—And in opera spheres
The "Girl" (the famed "Bohemian"),
And "Trovatore," held the ears,
    Gentlemen.

This season's paintings do not please,
    Gentlemen,
Like Etty, Mulready, Maclise;
Throbbing romance has waned and wanned;
No wizard wields the witching pen
Of Bulwer, Scott, Dumas, and Sand,
    Gentlemen.

The bower we shrined to Tennyson,
    Gentlemen,
Is roof-wrecked; damps there drip upon
Sagged seats, the creeper-nails are rust,
The spider is sole denizen;
Even she who read those rhymes is dust,
    Gentlemen!

We who met sunrise sanguine-souled,
    Gentlemen,
Are wearing weary. We are old;
These younger press; we feel our rout
Is imminent to Aïdes' den,—
That evening's shades are stretching out,
    Gentlemen!

And yet, though ours be failing frames,
    Gentlemen,
So were some others' history names,
Who trode their track light-limbed and fast
As these youth, and not alien
From enterprise, to their long last,
    Gentlemen.

Sophocles, Plato, Socrates,
    Gentlemen,
Pythagoras, Thucydides,
Herodotus, and Homer,—yea,
Clement, Augustin, Origen,
Burnt brightlier towards their setting-day,
    Gentlemen.

And ye, red-lipped and smooth-browed; list,
    Gentlemen;
Much is there waits you we have missed;
Much lore we leave you worth the knowing,
Much, much has lain outside our ken:
Nay, rush not: time serves: we are going,
    Gentlemen.

AFTER READING PSALMS

XXXIX., XL., ETC.

Simple was I and was young;
  Kept no gallant tryst, I;
Even from good words held my tongue,
  Quoniam Tu fecisti!

Through my youth I stirred me not,
  High adventure missed I,
Left the shining shrines unsought;
  Yet—me deduxisti!

At my start by Helicon
  Love-lore little wist I,
Worldly less; but footed on;
  Why? Me suscepisti!

When I failed at fervid rhymes,
  "Shall," I said, "persist I?"
"Dies" (I would add at times)
  "Meos posuisti!"

So I have fared through many suns;
  Sadly little grist I
Bring my mill, or any one's,
  Domine, Tu scisti!

And at dead of night I call:
  "Though to prophets list I,
Which hath understood at all?
  Yea: Quem elegisti?"

187–

"Cogitavi vias meas"
A cry from the green-grained sticks of the fire
   Made me gaze where it seemed to be:
'Twas my own voice talking therefrom to me
On how I had walked when my sun was higher—
   My heart in its arrogancy.

"You held not to whatsoever was true,"
   Said my own voice talking to me:
"Whatsoever was just you were slack to see;
Kept not things lovely and pure in view,"
   Said my own voice talking to me.

"You slighted her that endureth all,"
   Said my own voice talking to me;
"Vaunteth not, trusteth hopefully;
That suffereth long and is kind withal,"
   Said my own voice talking to me.

 "You taught not that which you set about,"
   Said my own voice talking to me;
"That the greatest of things is Charity. . . "
—And the sticks burnt low, and the fire went out,
   And my voice ceased talking to me.